TORN BETWEEN
TWO BROTHERS

VOLUME I

(2014 Print Edition)

by

Monique Farrow

Cover Design by: Dzine18

Published by: E-Ink It

Chapter One

Nothing got me wetter than fantasizing about getting pregnant. You could call me old fashioned, crazy, or just plain dumb. But it was all I thought about. In fact, my boo Darius was plunging deep inside my kitty from behind, while I cheered on his handsome swimmers in my mind. His massive hands wrapped around my tiny waist as he rhythmically beat it up. The shit was feeling so good, I purred in pleasure while teething his white Egyptian sheets. Greedily I threw my ass back, determined to take every inch of his manhood. I could feel my baby speeding up as I crossed my fingers, and hoped his players scored a goal. Darius slapped my ass, and the sound reverberated in his decked out master bedroom.

Turning around, I moaned, "I love you."

"I love you too." He grunted, before pulling out, and exploding onto my back.

"What the fuck, Darius! We're trying to get pregnant remember?" I jumped out of bed with a scowl on my face. Crossing my arms, I gave him the evil eye.

"Aw Fatty, I'm sorry. I forgot." He said, falling onto his back, satisfied and exhausted.

Standing over him, I seriously considered popping the shit out of him. But then, I surveyed his honey brown skin, ripped body, and super cute dimples, and changed my mind. Besides, we'd been together for over four years. Maybe it wasn't a long time to some, but it was more than long enough for me, because I desperately wanted a baby with him. For years, I wasted my time working at build a nigga work shop. Thank god, I resigned from that position, a long time ago. Finally I found a real man with ambition and drive. His money was good, his house was laid, and doors opened up where ever he went. He was definitely the type of man I wanted raising my children. I'd seen him carry the weight of the world on his shoulders without flinching. So I knew he could handle me and a baby, without a problem.

Darius was my personal genie. He gave me everything I ever asked for, except for what I really wanted. A ring and a baby. The ring, I could do without. Correction. Of course, I wanted a rock eventually. But for now, we could go down to the justice of the peace, and file some paper work. I wasn't picky. The baby on the other hand, I wanted asap. How could he forget, the most important thing to me. I'd been buying baby clothes, toys, and booties for over six months. I even had an entire room dedicated to baby at my place.

"Fatty. I forgot." He said, breaking my thoughts.

"Did you Darius? I thought we talked about this."

"We did. We're on the same page baby. I just forgot, damn. You forgive me?" He said, sitting on the edge of the bed in front of me, wearing the cutest pout I've ever seen.

"I guess. And one more thing. I told you, my name is Fatima, stop calling me Fatty. I don't like it."

"I don't like it. He mimicked, while scooping me up in his arms.

"What do you care, girl? You need some fat on your bones anyway. You're so tall and skinny."

"Skinny? Who you calling skinny." I played, punching him in the chest.

"If it wasn't for your tits and ass, you wouldn't have no meat on your bones."

"Good. That's exactly how I like it." I replied, mushing him with a pillow.

I got out of bed, tied my long coily hair in a bun, and grabbed my overnight bag, before heading towards the shower.

"You gonna join me." I asked, before leaving the room.

"In a minute. I gotta make a phone call." He looked a bit stressed which was unusual. Sex usually cleared his mind. We'd have to go another round in the shower. I didn't want him walking around uptight. It couldn't be healthy for his sperm. I wanted a relaxed happy baby, not a tiny tyrant.

"Don't be too long." I said, raising my brows.

"You serious? You know, I'm right behind you."

"You better be." I said, swaying my hips as I walked out the room. I didn't bother glancing over my shoulder to see if he was still watching. I knew he was. Darius couldn't help ogling my goodies.

Hot water fell onto my naked body as I thought about our relationship. Darius had been acting strange recently, and I couldn't figure out why. Last night, we went clubbing with my girl Tasha, and what I like to call her d.o.n, or dick on the night, and Darius hardly said anything. He didn't drink, laugh, or dance, and he always got turned up. Usually, I'm the sole designated driver, because I have a class of rowdy third graders to teach Monday through Friday. Last night was different. He was sipping ginger ale with me.

I tried to ignore the nagging voice in the back of my head saying he didn't want to start a family. I thought my dream of losing my virginity to the same man I'd raise a family with and marry was about to come true, but it seemed like he was getting cold feet. I planned to move in with him, after he committed to me by giving me a ring or baby. I preferred to get married first, but in reality no commitment could be stronger than a blood bond. We would always share a child. Even if, we didn't share a last name. Recently, he'd been pressuring me to move in, but I refused every time. I knew he loved me more than any other woman he'd ever been with in the past, because he told me so. But even the most patient man wouldn't wait forever. Maybe, he'd been acting strange, because I wouldn't move in yet.

"What was that?" I think I heard something. Turning off the water, I stuck my head out the shower door, and froze. I wasn't tripping. Whatever it was, I heard it again. I jumped out the shower, and put on my white cotton robe, before jetting down the staircase.

"Fuck that nigga." Darius yelled into his cell phone.

Downstairs was a mess. Every photo on the wall was crooked, or on the floor. A remote was sticking out the middle of the television screen hanging on the wall. His expensive leather couches were flipped on their backs. It looked like a cyclone ran through the middle of the living room.

"Baby what's going on."

Darius flipped his hand at me, and continued to talk. "How the fuck did he get caught? It was your responsibility to keep shit in line. Now, my ass is blowing in the wind."

Darius was acting like the Tasmanian Devil. He was throwing statues, books, and lamps. Practically, any and everything in his path was tossed across the room. I was stuck. I watched him destroy the house, silently. I'd seen him upset before, but never angry, and especially not psychotically enraged like this.

"250 grand! Nigga are you crazy? I don't have that kinda money. Who the fuck does this fool think he is? You better fix this shit."

Darius hurled his cell phone through the floor length window lining the entry way. He balled up his hands, and started pacing the floor, before slamming his fist against the masonry fireplace. Blood spilled from his knuckles, and down the length of his arms, but he kept at it.

"Baby what are you doing? Stop it! You're hurting yourself." I pleaded, running to his aid.

He ignored me, and continued to grunt and howl. It was like he was lost in a trance. I felt ghostly. He seemed blind, and deaf to everything I did. I grabbed his back, and attempted to pull him away. His elbow knocked me square in the nose, sending me careening back onto the floor.

"Oh shit! I'm sorry, baby. I'm sorry." He said, running to me on the floor.

Darius ripped his shirt in half. Then, he tore off a corner piece, and used it to stop my nose bleed. He rocked me in his arms, and kept telling me how sorry he was. Apparently, I needed to get hurt in order for him to hear me.

"Honey, its okay. What's going on?" I asked, concerned.

Sitting in front of me, he clasped both of my hands, and stared straight into my eyes. "I may have to serve some time." He said in one breath.

"You're going to prison?" I was horrified. I couldn't have heard him correctly. "What the hell are you talking about?"

He tightened his grip on my hands, and shook his head. He was irritated, but I was scared. I didn't know where all this was coming from. I tried to pull my hands from him, to wipe away the tears, but he wouldn't let me. It was like holding onto me gave him strength. "Babe. Just listen to me for a minute, damn. It's hard enough saying this shit, once. I won't repeat it, again."

I didn't disobey him. I never did. I just nodded, as tears streamed down my face. I was ready to listen.

"I think, I'm caught up. Eddie, my leg man, got snatched. The feds are putting steaks in front of him, trying to get him to eat. But according to my man, Tool, Eddie ain't biting, yet anyway. They're trying to get me for some work I put in last year. I can't go into the details. Just trust, I'm facing some serious time. According to Tool, Eddie will take the wrap. If, I keep him comfortable while he's serving time, down south. He wants 250 G's before his hearing date, which is about 90 days from now. Babe, I can't get locked up. And you know, I ain't got that kinda of money laying around. I spent all my reserves paying my lawyer for the last case, they were trying to pin on me."

I never saw Darius so scared in my life. He always had a plan A,B, and C. Now that I think about it, he was so good at what he did, I never heard about any business problems, until now.

"I've been trying to go legit. But nobody wants to give a nigga a chance. They want to check my work history, credit score, educational background, and some more shit. How the fuck, am I supposed to change my life around, if nobody will call me back to interview, let alone hire me?"

As I listened to Darius talk, I started thinking about the beginning of our relationship. I was so captivated by him. It didn't take long before I was handing over my V card. I met him during my freshman year at the University of Central Oklahoma. I was eighteen, and naive. He claimed to be in law school. I didn't question a word he said, because he oozed success from his nice clothes down to his sleek ride.

Eventually he told me, he was an entrepreneur into alternative business like the Italians. He wasn't hurting anybody like hustlers on the street slinging rock, running hoes, or knocking over banks. His business was different. He liked to say, he borrowed financial information from people who didn't need it anymore. He simply used social security numbers from dead and old people to finance a better life for himself. He constantly told me, he only committed victimless crimes, which technically didn't make it a crime at all. No one ever got hurt. But right about now, I felt like a victim, because my baby could be leaving me soon.

I was kicking myself for being so naive. I told him, I didn't want to know anything about what he did. As a result, I didn't have to deal with my conscious, and he didn't have to talk about his business. Up until today, the arrangement worked perfectly for both of us. Even when my girl, Tasha told me he was feared on the street. I didn't believe her, that's how much I was in denial. Darius was so syrupy sweet to me, and everyone I'd ever seen him around, I couldn't imagine him hurting a fly. Today, I saw the man she was talking about. I didn't know he was capable of getting so angry.

"Fatima. Are you even listening to me?" His irritated voice, snapped me out of my thoughts.

"Yes, D. I just don't know what to say. We were finally going to start our family. I'm just disappointed."

He was looking at me like I had shit on my face. "That's what you have to say to me, after all that?" He threw my hands, and stood up.

"Baby, wait don't be like that." I got up, and tried to comfort him.

"I'm worried about losing my freedom. Meanwhile, you're still on this baby shit. What the fuck is wrong with you? You think we should have a baby? Even in this situation? I'm starting to think you love my nut, more than me. Fuck you, the baby, and our engagement."

What he said hit me like daggers in the chest. "Darius. That came out wrong. I'm worried about you too, baby. I just thought we'd finally be happy. I can't help feeling a little disappointed."

"We'd finally be happy, or you, Fatima? Because, you're the only that's been pushing this shit, not me."

"What about us being on the same page. All that was bullshit, you said to me a minute ago?"

"No. That wasn't bullshit. This conversation is some bullshit. Matter-of-fact, I think you should leave?"

"Darius?" I pleaded.

10

He didn't respond. He just looked straight through me.

"You seriously want me to go?" I crossed my arms, and waited. "You're just going to kick me out your house, then?"

"Did I stutter? He said, staring me down.

I couldn't believe how hostile he was being. I looked around at the broken glass, trash, and leaning pictures on the wall, and realized it was probably for the best. I headed upstairs to get my bag, and accidentally found my reflection in the bathroom mirror. I looked terrible. My hair was a mess sitting on top of my head. Plus, I had dried blood hanging out my nose. The conversation downstairs was so heavy and dark, I completely forgot about my noise and the pain. He definitely was tripping.

I jogged downstairs ready to go, and saw Darius sitting on the couch with his head in his hands. He studied me, but didn't say anything. Obviously, there was something he wanted to say. So I stood at the bottom of the stairs and waited.

"I don't know what to say. So, I'm just going to say, see you later." He said, getting up to leave.

"Yeah. Whatever." I brushed past him, and through the front door.

Exhausted, I didn't want to say anything to stir

up a new conversation. We'd been together for years, and he never spoke to me the way he did today. I could actually say I was happy to leave. Thank god, I didn't get rid of my apartment. We had petty disagreements that were uncomfortable at worse, but never a true heated argument. Bickering and fighting has never been my style, I try to keep the peace. If our first fight was any indication of what was to come. I definitely wouldn't be sticking around for much longer. I'd leave his ass alone, first.

I jumped into my black 2008 Toyota Camry and backed out of his driveway. Funny, I remembered pulling into his house, hoping to have a little Darius, soon. Now, I didn't know where our relationship was headed, or what I'd gotten myself into.

Chapter Two

Tasha shot up, and the chair went flying behind her. "Girl, no that nigga didn't. He put his hands on you? Let me get my glock." She reached for an invisible gun in her coochie cut shorts. Then, she sat back down at the dining room table, shaking her head.

I sucked my teeth, and rolled my eyes. I was kicking myself for telling her crazy ass what happened. I loved Tasha. She was my girl, and the closest thing I had to family. But she simply did too damn much. Her ass didn't have a sling shot, let alone a gun. Her tiny apartment was cute, but it was no stage. Even though, she was putting on shows. I could picture her saying, "lights, camera, action" before her Oscar worthy performances, every time.

We met years ago, working at a local fast food joint. She was sixteen years old, and weeks away from having her second daughter, Nikki. Her mom stayed firm, and kicked her out after discovering she was pregnant again. She didn't want to help raise, Octavia, Tasha's oldest daughter let alone another child. Their relationship was, and still is awful. Me and Tasha were inseparable, because we both understood the struggle. I was awol from a girl's home, because living in the system became too much. At the time, we were both struggling to

13

get our own place which was a bitch. We've been family ever since.

"Girl, it couldn't have been me. I would have capped his ass." She said, snapping me out of my thoughts.

"Tasha, sit your butt down. And listen. The man didn't hit me. I told you, I ran into his elbow."

"Child boo" She said, waving her hand in my direction. "Don't we all, honey? I saw the same episode of Lucy, child. Next time, you'll be saying the door knob blacked your eye. I told you to get rid of that thirsty ass nigga. If a man seems to good to be true, it's because, he is."

My girl, had it out for Darius. On second thought, Tasha had it out for anyone with a penis. Of course, this time she had a valid reason to give him the side eye, but never before. You'd think she'd appreciate the gifts we give the kids. These bums out here, had my girl jaded. She thought every man was no good. She actually took pride in hustling them out of their money. A fair exchange was no robbery, according to her.

Tiny feet came pitter-pattering into the dining room. Nikki was so excited to talk, she knocked over Tasha's solo cup of gin, and my cup of apple juice. Tasha could definitely handle her liquor, unlike me. I couldn't even tell she'd been drinking.

"Damn. Nikki. Watch where you're going."

"Sorry Mama."

"What is it girl?"

"Tavia hit Daddy right in his eyeball." She said, pretending to get hit herself in the face.

I couldn't help laughing. The child certainly had her mother's flair for drama. As if on cue, DeMarcus came walking into the kitchen holding his eye with dried streams stuck on his face. He was the youngest of Tasha's three kids. They were all stair steps. Octavia was seven, Nikki was six, and DeMarcus was four years old.

"Girl hold on a minute."

I already knew what was coming next. She went into the back room with a fly swatter. Tasha definitely didn't believe in sparing the rod, or spoiling the child. I could hear Octavia crying out in pain as Tasha lashed her for hitting her little brother. My heart silently cried with her. Her aching voice reminded me of all the times, I was beaten as a child. Growing up in the system wasn't easy. In fact, it was a living nightmare. Sometimes, I didn't think I would make it till eighteen. I regularly thought about taking myself. Believing no one would miss me anyway. I took a moment to thank god for bringing Darius and Tasha into my life. Even though, I disagreed with her parenting, I knew better than to tell a parent how to raise their child. That was one of the first lessons I learned as a new teacher, this year.

DeMarcus climbed up on my lap, and instantly sweetened my thoughts. I just wanted to eat him up. Damn, I wanted a child so bad. He gazed up at me with his big doe eyes, and I swear, I almost melted off the chair.

"Hi Aunty Fatty," he said, rubbing his eye, and laying his head against my chest." My eyes stung when he called me Fatty, I couldn't help thinking about my boo. What would I do, if he got locked up? He'd been my life for the last four years. I prayed he was okay.

"Boy get down." Tasha said, shooing him away with the fly swatter.

"That boy is always in your face."

"Don't be messing with my baby. You know me and Darius, love having him over." I said, laughing and kissing him in his dimpled cheek. Tasha didn't like me bringing him to Darius's house. But I insisted he needed a male remodel, and she couldn't disagree. DeMarcus jumped down, and ran into the back room, while Tasha made herself comfortable at the table again.

Looking across the table, I thought about how hard my friend's life must be. She was only nineteen years old, and on her third child, which is why I regularly took the kids. I liked taking the stress off her shoulders every once and awhile. I knew she needed a break every once, and awhile. I especially enjoyed watching little man. He was the closest thing I had to a baby. Besides, Darius liked seeing me in my element because, he didn't have to hear about me wanting a baby. When I was content taking care of DeMarcus. I smiled thinking about our little play dates.

"I know. I know. He's so cute. And all that shit. You can take his ass, if you want. Anyway, lets get back to the tea. So, he busted your nose, and then what happen." She said, peering at me from across the table. Sometimes, I couldn't stand her butt.

I picked up my juice, and rolled my eyes at her high yellow ass, before going on with the story.

"Anyway, he ran into some really bad business problems, that sent him over the edge. The argument wasn't even about us or having a baby. He's emotions just got the best of him."

I love my girl Tasha, but I can't put his business out in the street. I wasn't about to tell her butt, everything, in case he was able to feed the bird, in order to stay out of jail. All she needed to know is that he didn't want to have a baby anymore.

"I knew he was one of those Wall Street types. Money ain't everything child. If he loses his business, what's he going to do, girl? Throw himself out the window." She said, cackling.

"Its not about the business, my nose, or money. I want to have a baby. And now he's saying he doesn't want to. In fact, he said he didn't want to get married either."

"What's your problem girl? You know he was just talking out of his ass. He still loves you. Have some faith. Besides, kids aren't that great, believe me. You're 22 years old, you have plenty of time for babies. Enjoy yourself. Shit, you can take one, or all of mine. I'll even give you a discount. Take one, get the other pair free. While supplies last." She said, half joking. We both cracked up.

I couldn't help feeling a little pissed off. How was she going to be such a hypocrite. She had three people to love. I just wanted one little person to call my own. If she wasn't my sister, I'd check her ass. She knew, how sensitive I was about this topic. I thought, she'd understand. It felt like I was the only member on Team Baby.

Chapter Three

My kids really tried me today. They were so bad. I stopped and wondered, why I even decided to become a teacher. I must have lost my mind. The muscles in the back of my neck tightened, and my head screamed for Tylenol, as I drove home after a long day's work. All I could do was imagine myself falling into my California king sized bed, with a remote in hand, prepared to watch a few hours of ratchet reality television in order to release some stress. I hadn't checked in on Joseline, Stevie J, and Mimi in awhile. They always seemed to be a good distraction, which I desperately needed, after the last few days.

Pulling into my reserved parking space, I looked up, and my heart almost leaped out my chest. The lights were on inside my apartment. How the hell was that possible? Did I forget to turn them off? Maybe, I did. No. That's impossible. I remembered turning them off before leaving for work in the morning. In fact, I double checked.

Cutting off my car engine, I sat and thought about what to do. I'd watched one too many episodes of the First 48 to go upstairs unarmed, and ill prepared. I opened my glove compartment and stared at the little handgun, Darius gave me. He told me to carry it around just in case, some fool wanted to try something stupid, but I never touched the thing. I never dreamed, I would have to use it. I couldn't help wracking my brain with possible scenarios. Who could be up there? Maintenance, maybe? I knew, I didn't give anyone a key to my house. My home was my sanctuary, I rarely invited anyone over. I preferred going out in public, or at the other person's spot, instead of my own. Darius, didn't even have a key. I planned on giving him one, after we got married. Taking a deep breathe, I put the gun in my bag using my thumb and index finger. Whoever it was, was in for a surprise.

As I climbed my building staircase, the knot in my stomach grew wider and wider. Suddenly, I realized my stressful day was only going to get worse. When I reached my front door, I saw a black bag on the floor with a note attached to front. It read:

Dear Fatty,

I'm sorry about the other day. You know you're my everything. My future wife, and mother of my children. I shouldn't have spoken to you the way I did. I'm sorry. Look inside the bag, I bought you something special, to let you know just how much I love and miss you. There's more waiting for you, on the other side of the door.

Love Darius.

The note was sweet and everything, but how did

he get inside my house? I'm sure, I didn't give him a key. After the argument we had the other day, he didn't call, which really surprised me. Even though, I wasn't sure where we stood, I thought about calling him, practically every second of the day. But decided against it, because I wasn't about to teach him, his behavior was okay. His silence made me feel relieved, I didn't give him full access to my place. The other day had me second guessing our relationship, because I couldn't, and didn't fight.

Reading the note again, I dropped my shoulders, rolled my neck slowly, and realized none of that mattered now, because apparently, swatting my hands, and biting my tongue worked. Since he felt bad enough to arrange such a sweet apology.

I peered down at the bag, sitting in front of my feet. I couldn't help wondering if it was finally the ring, I'd been waiting for? I held my breath, and my pulse quickened, as I eagerly searched inside.

"Lingerie?" I said, letting out a sigh.

I guess, money wasn't what it used to be. I picked up the bag, and walked inside.

"Oh my god, baby." I squealed, holding my chest.

Darius had completely out done himself. There was an assortment of white candles arranged throughout my living room. Joe's I Wanna Know was playing in the background, and petals were scattered on the floor, but he was no where to be found. I dropped the bag and searched for him in my future baby's bedroom, and my own, but didn't find him. I could see the master bathroom door was open, from my bedroom doorway. I walked inside, and found him standing in nothing but a white towel with a glass of champagne in his hand. Slung over his arm was a towel and luffa. The bath water was drawn, and I could see he had my favorite body wash and lotion sitting on the ledge of the tub. I couldn't help noticing how delicious he looked.

"Welcome home." he said, flashing those dimples I love while surveying my body.

"Hi baby. You did all this for me?"

"Of course, I did. You deserve it." He said, but he seemed distracted.

"Babe. Did someone steal your shit. I left a bag and note in front of the door?" He asked, cracking his knuckles. He was gearing up to fight.

"No, honey. I got it. Thank you." I said readily, not wanting him to blow up again.

Maybe he was irritated, but not upset. Either way, I wanted to keep him calm, whenever I could. The fight changed something inside me. It was like I was waiting for the monster to show up again. I wanted to ask, how he got inside my apartment, but it didn't seem like the right time. So, I decided to ask later.

"Let me take care of you." He said, proceeding to undress me from head to toe.

Exhausted, I let him. Our problems could wait, for now. I stepped into the bathtub, and relaxed for the first time all day. I was nice absorbing the moment. At first, we sat quietly, as he worked out all the kinks in my neck and shoulders. Then, I asked the huge question looming in the room.

"Did you fix your business problem, baby?" He must have, why else would he be in such a good mood?

"I thought you'd never ask."

"Daddy's got everything figured out." He said, kissing the back of my neck.

"Hmm, that feels good. Tell me everything."

"Are you sure you want to know?" He said, stalling with a smile in his voice.

"Boy don't play. Tell me, what's up."

"Well, my dad passed away, last week."

Shocked. I spun around in the tub, splashing him in the face.

"Damn. Babe. Watch out." He said, falling back laughing.

"Excuse me?"

"Did I hear you correctly. Your dad dying is good news?" I knew my face looked crazy. But I couldn't help it. I was genuinely shocked. I couldn't believe what he was saying. Was he really happy his dad was dead? I knew Darius put on a strong face, but I would've at least expected him to be a little sad.

"Look. I'm not happy the man is dead. I'm happy, I found a solution to our problems. So chill."

"How's that?" I asked, with raised eyebrows.

"My dad didn't flash his money, but I know he wasn't broke. He was all about his paper. There's no way he didn't have a fat life insurance policy somewhere. He was always teaching me and Marcus to save half of what we earned, and shit like that. Plus, I got a phone call today, telling me to meet with his lawyer tomorrow about his will. His death was a blessing in disguise. I needed 250 grand, right around the time he crocks. So, from where I'm standing, it looks like he was watching over me, without even knowing it? Damn, babe. I thought you'd be happy." He said, throwing his hands up.

Honestly, happy was the last emotion I'd use to describe how I felt, at the moment. I understood, Darius needed the money to stay out of jail.

Obviously, I didn't want him getting arrested. But, it would be wrong for me to jump up and down, over a man's death. I've never met his dad, or anyone else in his family, now that I think about it. So hearing about his death, before hearing stories about Christmas or birthdays, seemed off.

"Honey. Of course, I'm happy." I lied. I knew better than to stifle his happiness. Besides, I didn't want to mess up the good vibe we had going.

"Fatty, you're a horrible liar. What's the problem?" He said, sitting on the side of the tub with his arms crossed.

"I don't know. I don't want to be happy about someone dying. It's not right. It almost feels evil."

"Evil? You think, I'm a bad guy?" He asked, looking hurt.

"Of course not. Don't be silly. I know you're a good man. I wouldn't be with you, if I thought you weren't. I just don't know what to think about the whole situation."

Dropping his towel, he joined me in the tub. I turned around, and placed my head on the front of his shoulder.

"I'll tell you what to think." He said, rubbing the center of my sweet spot.

"Think about what kind of dress you'll be wearing, when we walk down the isle, because I'm not going anywhere."

I enveloped the warm sensation taking over my body, because I wanted to believe every word, dripping from his lips. I placed my negative thoughts in box, deep inside the depths of my mind.

"Go on." I said, lost in the dream.

Rubbing my belly, he went on. "You should also rethink your digs. Since, you'll be too big to wear those skinny jeans, and cute clothes you like. I'm going to have you woddeling around this joint soon."

"Oh. Is that right?" I said, turning around, looking deeply into his eyes.

"Darius. Don't lie to me, if you don't mean it. I want to know the truth."

"I'm serious as a heart attack." He said, pulling me onto his manhood.

I wasn't getting any sleep tonight. That was for damn sure. He had me so open, I forgot to ask about his accomplice threatening to squeal.

Chapter Four

I threw my napkin on the bistro table. I was pissed. I stopped myself from cussing out the waitress. Even though, she technically didn't do anything wrong. Besides annoy the hell out of me. Since, she came to my table at least four times within the last twenty minutes, asking if I was ready to order. I told her non-listening behind, I would call her when I was ready. But apparently, she didn't understand English very well. Even though, she looked like a so called all American girl, whatever the hell that means?

"Ma'am, we really need this table, if you're not going to order something soon." She returned.

Grabbing the sides of the table, I took a deep breathe, and exhaled. I needed to calm down, because I really wanted to scream. Truth be told, she had every right to keep coming back. The place was jam packed. People were rushing to grab a bite to eat, before heading back to work. I understood, everyone needed to get paid, especially minimum waged workers. Unfortunately, the state didn't pay me much better than them. So, I couldn't afford to order expensive lunches to eat alone. My real problem was dumb ass, Darius. Not her. He was supposed to be here over an hour ago. At first, I waited outside, hoping his car would pull into the parking lot soon, but then it started to rain. So I decided to take a seat.

"Ma'am." she said, disturbing my thoughts.

"We need this table."

"Fine." I said, gathering my things to leave.

Darius definitely had some explaining to do. If he wasn't dead, incarcerated, or in the hospital. I truly felt sorry for his ass, because I'm ready to set it off. I understood, he had a lot on his mind, but that was no excuse to treat me bad. I planned on giving him more than a piece of my mind. Because, this madness had to stop. I didn't know who he thought he was, standing me up. Sitting in the middle of the restaurant alone wasn't only annoying, it was embarrassing.

"What the hell is the problem now?" I said, aloud.

As I pulled into my complex, I could see his car in my reserved parking space, I paid extra for every month. Begrudgingly, I found an inconvenient place to park far away from my front door. I expected a damn good excuse, because I was more than tired of his bullshit. How could we start a family, if I couldn't even count on him showing up for lunch? Why couldn't he be the responsible business man, I met two years ago? If I was honest with myself, I could admit secretly I hoped the candles, music, and lingerie was a sign the old Darius was back. But obviously, his butt wasn't ready to return. Since the dumb shit kept on rolling.

At the top of the staircase, there was no Darius. This fool had to be sitting in my apartment. I knew I should have asked how he got into my place, the last time he was over. Now I had to deal with these surprise pop ups. Plus, he had the audacity to kick me out of his spot. Meanwhile he had full access to mine. Uh uh, things had to change. I told him, as soon as we met, I didn't want to move in together without being married. He was mad at first, but I thought he understood, and got over it. Of course, he called me crazy, since we had sex, and were always together. I didn't want him having a key to my place, until I had a commitment. Somehow the terms of our relationship changed, without me knowing. I had to reset everything, before shit got too far out of hand.

With my attitude fully intact, I threw open the front door, ready to duke it out. Immediately, I realized I had a much bigger problem than I expected. Darius was slumped in front of my suede couch with a bottle of Jack tightly gripped in his hand. Instantly, my eyes popped open, I dropped everything, and cupped my mouth in shock. He looked a hot mess. The rims of his eyes were red, and the lids were swollen, it appeared he'd been crying.

"Baby. What's the matter?" I said, rushing over to see what was wrong.

"Fuck that nigga. Fuck em. I hope his ass is frying, where ever he is." He said, slurring his words, while trying to stand up.

"Sit down baby. Relax. Tell me what's wrong." I said, pushing his shoulders down.

"The fuck you think? That nigga don't love me. He never did. Nobody gives a fuck about Darius. It's Marcus they love." He said, punching himself in the face.

"Stop it. What the hell are you doing?"I screamed. I'd never seen him like this before. He looked so broken, and confused. What the hell was he drinking? Lighter fluid. I couldn't believe my eyes. He never acted this way. Darius was always strong and well put together. I didn't know the person, in front of me, or where they came from.

"What do you care? You don't care about me. You just want a baby. You don't love me." He said, beginning to cry. He words trailed off, but I got the gist. My baby had finally cracked under the pressure. I held him tightly against my breast, as he cried it out. I didn't know what else to do. But I knew one thing, I wasn't going to abandon him, during his time of need. I knew exactly what it felt like to be alone in this world, full of opportunists and vultures ready to feast on you in a vulnerable moment. I was determined to be the woman he needed me to be no matter what. We were going to make it through whatever was causing him to crack up like this. He was more than my man, he was the only family I had besides, Tasha. Eventually, his tears stopped falling, and it felt safe to break the silence.

"Did Eddie take the deal? Is that why you're upset, baby?" I asked, gently.

"No. Not yet. But he will."

"Don't say that. We don't know that yet."

"You're so fucking stupid. Wake up. I can't come up with the money. It's over. I'm going to jail." He snapped.

"We don't know that. Stop speaking against yourself. Let's stay positive. What did his lawyer say?" I said, choosing to ignore the daggers he threw at me. It must be the sauce talking, not him.

"He said, my dad doesn't give a fuck about me. He didn't leave me shit. Is that what you want to hear?" He said, staggering onto his feet. He tilted his head back, and took another swig. I wanted to stop him, but my intuition told me not to. One wrong move, and he'd be swing on me, instead of himself.

"My dad, didn't leave me shit. But, he left $500,000 to my brother. He could have split it

31

down the middle. Half is exactly what I needed. But no. You know what the muthafucker left me? A bible. A motherfucking bible." He said, laughing so hard it brought him to tears.

"Can you believe that shit? I'm his oldest son. I'm his goddamn junior. Not Marcus. I'm his fucking son too. What about me?" He roared, as if I was his dad, instead of his girl. Stumbling back, he fell onto his left leg and took another drink.

"Marcus doesn't even need the shit. He's a fucking doctor."

Quietly, I watched on the couch as he spiraled into a dark place, I didn't want to visit. I had no idea where the night was headed. I'd learned more about him, his father, and his brother, than I ever knew before. Every time, I tried to ask him about his family in the past, he would change the subject. I figured, it was too painful to talk about like parts of my childhood. I totally understood wanting to move up and foreword.

Punching, nothing but air, he started screaming, "I'm sorry. I didn't meant it." over and over again.

"Baby, what did you do? Why are you sorry." Was all I could get out from across the room. I stayed planted on the couch as tears of sadness and frustration streamed from my eyes. I wanted to hold him, and tell him everything was going to be okay, but I was too afraid. I didn't know what he would do next. He fell onto his knees, and cried in the middle of my living room floor. I could tell he was exhausted. Slowly, I slid onto the floor in front of the couch. I wanted him to know he wasn't alone.

"Tell me what happened baby. I want to help you feel better. Let it out."

"I killed him."

I sucked in a deep breathe, and held it. I didn't want to show him, how much what he said, shocked and frightened me. I knew Darius committed white collar crimes. But murder. It took me over a year to accept he stole financial information from dead people and the elderly. But murder, I didn't think I could swallow. I wasn't prepared to hear the words coming out of his mouth. His eyes were surveying my reaction, they felt like beams burning into my skin. Gradually, I let my chest fall. Hoping my surprise didn't register on my face. I didn't say anything. I just waited for him to continue, as he set cradling his head in his hands.

"I was just a little kid. I don't know how it happened." He paused, and looked at me like he was deciding whether to continue. The truth was, he had no choice, because the words had already been spoken. He'd have to tell me now or later, because, never was no longer an option.

"We were supposed to stay inside, but I didn't listen. I snuck out anyway, without my parent's permission."

"Fuck. Why didn't I listen." He continued with hot streams running down his face.

"Even then, he was the better son. All my parents talked about was Marcus is so smart, Marcus is going to follow in Big D's footsteps, Why can't Darius be more like Marcus? The shit never stopped. No matter what I did. I could never be better than him. So, I stopped trying. If they didn't want to see the good in me, I'd show them how bad I could be."

In that moment, I realized I didn't want him to continue. There was no doubt in my mind Darius was the man for me. But our relationship wasn't the same after his explosion the other day. I still loved him, but my view of him was different. He no longer was my pillar of strength. Seeing him out of control and fragile, woke me up to reality. I built him up in my mind. His ability to survive in difficult situations hooked me to him. I unfairly made him out to be a super hero, because I needed one at the time. Now, he needed me. I wasn't sure if I could be there for him in the same way, because his problems were so huge, and larger than life, but I was going to try. I continued to listen to his confession, and prayed I could handle whatever he was going to say next.

"Eric loved me. He loved everyone, but

especially me. He looked at me like I was super human. Everywhere I went, he wanted to go. He was my sidekick, until that night. Everyone wanted to go to the fair, including me, but my parents said no. Instead of listening, I woke up, grabbed my bag, full of soda and snacks I prepared earlier, and headed out. Unfortunately, Eric woke up before I could get out the window. He wanted to come along. I was just a kid, too. I was thirteen years old. I just wanted to have fun with everyone else. I didn't want anyone to get hurt. I tried to tell him he was too little and needed to stay. But he was persistent like most 7 years old. He wouldn't take no for an answer. He put on his shoes, because he wanted to go too. He was so excited to go with his big brother. If he only he knew, what I had planned for him. I told him to be quiet, so we didn't wake up the rest of the house. Marcus was asleep in the room too. I didn't want Jesus himself to wake up. Unfortunately, the piece of shit stayed asleep. God, why didn't he wake up? If anyone shouldn't be here, it was him, not Eric. He could have stopped me. God, why didn't he stop me."

I held myself so tightly, my fingers began to tingle. I couldn't process what he was saying. Eric? Who the hell was Eric? And why didn't he tell me about him sooner? Darius never told me he had another brother until tonight? He told me about Marcus, his mom, and his dad. I could tell the conversation was headed in a dark direction. I wanted him to stop. It seemed like talking about it helped him control his emotions. So, there was no way, I was going to interrupt.

"We had a blast at the fair. We ate Now or Laters, Cry Babies, Kit Kats, and drank grape soda all night. Eric said, he never had so much fun. It was really a night to remember." He eyes teared up and he took a breathe. It was obviously hard for him to continue.

"We walked home. It must have been at least 11 o'clock. Eric kept lagging behind. I was tired, I kept telling him to catch up. I'd stop for a few seconds, but didn't carry him. Instead, I let him fall behind. Eventually, we reached the train tracks. It was only two blocks from our house. He was so far behind, I could barely see him. By the time, I heard the sound of the train. I realized I couldn't see him anymore. I tried to reach him. I turned back around." Streams started running down the length of his face. I tried to put my arms around him, but he pulled back.

"Damn it. Fatty. I need to say this. I turned back around. I ran as fast as I could. But he was gone. The train drug him for miles. When I got back, he was nothing but broken bones, cartilage, and mangled flesh. It was my fault. They were right. I'm a piss of shit." Darius started hitting the sides of his face. He completely lost. I ran to him, forcing my arms around him. If he was going to hurt himself, he could hit me too. I wasn't about watch him self destruct anymore. Luckily, as soon as I did, he stopped. I held him for the rest of the night, until he fell asleep.

Chapter Five

I hardly got any sleep. Seeing Darius fall to pieces in front of my eyes, really woke me up to some hardcore truths. All this time, he'd been focused on me, without taking care of himself. He bought my car, paid my rent, and took me shopping amongst other things while carrying such a heavy burden alone. Meanwhile, he was living in his own personal hell, and I wasn't even aware. What type of partner was I, if I didn't even know he was suffering? I was disgusted with myself. I should have known he needed me. I couldn't help feeling selfish, which was why I was going to doing everything in my power to make it up to him.

As soon as the sun peeked over the clouds, I was zipping around the house. All morning, I'd been cleaning and rearranging furniture to clear my mind. I was determined to find a solution to his problems before he woke up. He'd been a pillar of strength for me in the past. Now it was my turn to do the same for him. If outside influences were going to try to bring my baby down, I'd have to dilute their effects by being twice as positive, and encouraging. He obviously needed my help keeping his head above water. So, that was exactly what I was going to do. After spending a few hours thinking about everything that's transpired over the last few weeks, I found a good solution to our problems. I just hoped he would go along with my plan.

I placed a fresh pair of folded black lounge pants and a crisp white tee shirt on the foot of the bed, before heading back to the kitchen. He was still nestled in dream world, unaware of what I had planned for him once he woke up. The smoked ham I was sizzling in a cast iron skillet, while I scrambled four eggs in the pan next door. I had a bowl of pancake batter resting on the counter top, too. It would be ready to throw on the hot griddle as soon as he walked into the kitchen. Today was going to be a good day for him no matter what. Nothing was going to ruin it, if I had anything to say about it.

"Hmm, what's that smell?" He asked, walking into the room while rubbing his belly.

"Breakfast for a king of course. I've got smoked ham, scrambled eggs, and buttermilk pancakes on the way." I said, pouring the pancake batter onto the hot griddle. I jogged over, and placed a soft kiss on his lips. Then asked, "How'd you sleep?"

"Damn, baby. I knew, I had good taste." He said, showing off his deep dimples. He wrapped his arm around my waist, and pulled me into a deep kiss. I knew my baby was grateful without him saying a word. His sweet kiss was all the thanks I needed. I quickly ran around the breakfast bar to flip the pancakes before they burned.

"Babe, about last night."

"Uh uh, today is a new day. Do you really want to talk about last night?" I said, placing his food and a glass of orange juice in front of him, with a skeptical look on my face.

He smiled at me from the bar and said, "You're amazing, girl. I don't know how I got so lucky."

"We're meant to be together. Luck has nothing to do with it."

Looking at him I could see, he was in a much better mood. I didn't want to drag down the day by focusing on last night. As far as, I was concerned yesterday was dead, gone, and irrelevant. There was no point in talking about it now. We just needed to move on, and forward.

"I don't want to talk about the past, but I do want to discuss our future. You up for it?" I asked, not wanting to push to soon.

"Shoot."

"Well, I've been thinking about our predicament. I know you have a potentially pending case we can stop by paying Eddie. But that doesn't look possible at the moment. So, I've been thinking of alternative plans. I think I have a good one, that can keep us together and you out of jail."

"Did I wake up in heaven? Because you're answering all my prayers without me even asking. He said, laughing.

"Shush. I'm serious." I said, placing my finger over his lips.

"We may not have money at the moment, but he have time, and a heads up. So, lets make the best of it. We could sell everything. Your house, my car, our clothes, everything but a few necessity items. Then, we can clear out our accounts. Before heading out of town. I know I've been waiting to have a little Darius for the longest, but not if that means I have to lose you. Having you home with me is more important than anything else. We will need to get married though. So if worse case scenario happens, we wouldn't have to testify against each other.

Darius sat back, and contemplated what I said. I couldn't tell from his expression what he was thinking. I just crossed my fingers and hoped he would think it was a good plan. He got up from the bar stool, and grabbed both of my hands.

"Fatima, I appreciate you trying to help fix the situation. I really do. I couldn't ask for more. But my problems are little more complicated than that. I can't just get up and leave. The type of business I do, isn't hard to track, when somebody has the inside scoop. Plus, there are cameras on practically

41

every street corner these days. Where could we go without anyone seeing us get there. The camera nowadays are so good they can count the money in your hands from across the room."

Dropping my shoulders, I began to shed a few tears. I knew my idea was a stretch, but I couldn't think of anything else to do. Darius swept away the tears on my cheek and held me close. For the first time in awhile, I allowed myself to relax in his embrace.

"I don't want you worry about us, and definitely not me. I'm may have been down for a minute, but I'm still the man. I can take care of us. You don't have to worry. I've found a solution to our problem, but you'll have to keep an opened mind." I raised my forehead off his shoulders, eager to hear his plan.

"Tell me. We have to do something. We can't just sit on our hands, because I don't know what I'd do, if you weren't home with me." Darius pecked my lips and led me to the living room couch. We both set down while he held my hands.

"I'll need your support to make this plan work. But, I'm just not sure you'll agree to help me." He said, rubbing his forehead with one hand.

"Are you crazy. Have I not proven, I'm here for you enough? Of course, I'll help. I'll do anything to keep you safe, and at home. Now tell me."

"I'm not sure you can, because you're not about this life. You didn't even want to be with me when I told you about my business. It almost tore us apart. I don't know if you can handle doing what it takes to get me out of this situation.

"Darius, I don't know what to tell you. I've accepted your business and way of life, which is why I'm still sitting here. I'm older and wiser now. I understand life isn't fairy dust and unicorns. Sometimes you have to step outside the lines to get what you need. I get that now. You're my family. If I have to make sacrifices in the short term to have you in the long term, so be it. I'll do whatever it takes to keep you home. So we can have the family we've always wanted.

"Good. Because I have a fail proof plan, but you're gonna have to be smart enough to think outside the box. You can't be like most women who operate off of emotion. You'll have to do what it takes to get us out of this situation. I know you have a good head on your shoulders. I'm just not sure, if you trust me.

"Stop slow playing Darius. Of course, I trust you. Just tell me what I can do to help."

"We can't get 250 G's in two months, because I'm too hot right now. I can't risk getting caught. And nobody wants to do business with me for obvious reason. Which is why, my dad's life insurance policy was my last shot."

"Right."

"Well, I've got a back a plan."

"Go on."

"Marcus has 500 G's coming in about the same time. He doesn't know anything about me, but I know plenty about him. I've done a thorough background check on him. And my brother isn't hurting for money."

"So, you"re going to ask him for your half?"

"No. You are."

"I am? He doesn't even know me."

"That's why it's perfect. Here me out."

"Marcus is a chump. He doesn't know shit about shit. The only thing he's ever known is how to read a book. The kid has no street smarts or common sense. I think his ass is autistic, or something. Point is. We can easily con him out of his money."

"How can we con him? I don't know anything about conning somebody. Plus, I don't feel comfortable doing that."

"So, you won't do anything for us to be together."

"Darius. That's not what I said."

"Then what are you saying?" Darius was

44

starring me down. He was disappointed in my response. I just didn't know what to say, because I wasn't expecting him to bring up his brother. I wasn't lying when I said, I'd do anything for us to be together. I just didn't see how us both committing crimes, would stop him from getting arrested.

"I can't commit crimes. I'm a school teacher. That would ruin my career, if I got caught. Plus I don't see how me becoming a criminal, keeps you out of jail.

"Fatty, you're my girl. I would never ask you to do anything that could get you arrested." Relived, I let out a heavy sigh.

"I don't know how to say this. So, I'm just going to come out with it. I need you to hustle my brother."

"Hustle him? Hustle him. You mean, you want me to have sex with your brother?

"I mean, I want you to get what we need, however you can. If that means sex okay, but of course, any other way would be better."

I just sat there with my mouth open. I didn't have any words to express how I felt. I just sat there and stared at him.

"Look. I know it's a lot to take in. I wouldn't ask, if there was any other way. Believe me. I don't want my girl to be with anyone else, but this is the only way for us to have what we want. After you get the money, I'll be free. We can get married, and have the baby you've always wanted. Just think about it. I know, you'll make the right decision.

"I'm going to wash up. You can join me if you want." Darius stood up and walked towards the bathroom. Stunned. I sat on the couch, alone, trying to figure out how my life became such a mess. Never in a million years did I think Darius would ask me to sleep with another man, let alone his own brother.

Chapter Six

Driving to Tasha's house seemed like a trip around the world, since it felt like the earth stopped spinning, and the sun didn't come out, after what Darius asked me to do. Apart of me, felt like he was being the logical go getter, I fell in love with several years ago. It sounds crazy on the surface, but what he said did make a lot of sense. There was no way to keep him with me, if we couldn't come up the 250 grand. Hell, I wouldn't take the wrap for free if I was Eddie, either. Besides, his brother got more than his share of their father's life insurance policy. The fact his dad chose to punish him, even in death, for a mistake he made as a child was disgusting in my opinion. He should have split everything down the middle, instead of leaving Marcus everything. Plus, the bible was an unnecessary fuck you to boot. I could only assume, Darius thought we'd live happily ever after, if I went along with his plan. But of course, that was wishful thinking because life never goes according to plan.

I hated to admit it, but I understood where he was coming from. Darius was just being his typical analytical self. I used to love the fact he was unemotional and direct, when making important decisions. Everything usually turned out good, because of his unique perspective on things. I actually thought, his unemotional view of the world was more balanced than my sometimes fanciful way of thinking. But now, it was coming back to bite me on the ass. I didn't know what to do. A large part of me couldn't believe he loved me, if he'd let me sleep with another man, regardless of the situation. Because we could always start where we left off, if he did get arrested. Had I known, he was going to ask me to do something so crazy, I wouldn't have went on about being willing to do anything to keep him out of jail. Now, I felt obligated to follow through.

I sat inside my car in front of Tasha's apartment and spaced out for a bit. My mind was overdue for a break. The kids were running and playing outside, like they were having the time of their life. Octavia was chasing DeMarcus and Nikki with a water hose, while I let my thoughts roam to a better place. I smiled enviously, as I watched them play freely. If only I could leave my problems behind, and join them. I could see Tasha sitting on the porch beating a pack of cigarettes against her palm. It didn't look like she was in a good mood from were I was sitting, which was strange because she usually was.

"Your highness, are you going to join me on the porch." She asked, dramatically taking a bow.

"I was just admiring the kids. I'm right behind you." I said, grabbing my purse and water bottle.

48

We settled into our sits on her front porch. Tasha popped a fresh Newport 100 in her mouth, as we watched them play. It was a typical gorgeous June summer day. Neighbors were out playing bones, drinking beer, bumping music, and hanging out. Witnessing the carefree spirit around me only made me feel worse. I couldn't help wondering how the hell things got so bad?

"What's the matter? Darius didn't buy you another car?" Tasha laughed, sarcastically.

I hated when Tasha acted like my life was a bed of roses. Yes, I didn't have three children that I raised alone, but that was intentional, not accidental. I could have easily been her, if I focused on getting ahead, instead of getting my education. Single mother's like her drove me crazy with their tiny violins and sob stories. True. Tasha had been through some things, but I had too. She should be trying to figure out how to get a job. Instead of what my man was or wasn't doing for me. It really shouldn't have been any of her concern.

"Girl, how you been? You know I'm just a little tipsy. I don't mean no harm."

I cut my eyes at her, cleared my throat and said, "Things have been a little rough lately. I was hoping to get some advice from my sister. But, if you're too lit to talk. Let me know, I have no problem moving around."

"Go ahead girl, I'm sorry. It ain't nothing but the devil in this cup, causing me to act like that. I got it together now." She said, straightening her shirt, and sitting up right.

"Darius has been going through somethings. I failed to mention he was being blackmailed, the last time I saw you. That's why he lost it the other day. One of his partners, got arrested recently, and he is threatening to tell his business, if he doesn't come up with some serious cash."

Tasha grabbed her stomach and fell over laughing. She wiped away tears with the back of her hand, she was cracking up so much. Catching her breath she said, "Child, everybody knows Darius's ain't nobody's boss, or business man. You're the only fool dense enough to believe anything said to you. The whole city knows he is a hustler in a suit and tie, your dumb ass is the only one out of the loop. I swear, you're as late as a ho on Sunday morning. I been knowing the business. I'm just glad your ass, finally decided to tell me the truth."

I watched, as someone I consider my sister, made light of my situation. I thought about my limited resources, and my eyes began to sting. Tasha and Darius were my support system, but neither were being very good to me at the moment. I came over expecting her to offer me some sound advice and direction. If I knew she was going to be so ruthless and cold, I would have saved my gas and stayed home. Losing my man, dream, and way of life was bad enough, without having her laugh about it. So I gathered my things to leave. I wasn't about to let her make my already difficult situation worse.

"Fatima … Fatima? Where are you going girl? You can't take a joke? She said, tugging on my wrist.

"I don't have time for games, today. If you're not going to be my sister by helping me, I'm gonna leave. I don't have time for your mess."

Tasha cleared her throat, and patted the chair next to her. "Fatima, your right. I shouldn't be making fun of you. I won't drink anything until we figure this situation out." I looked at her sideways, but sat down.

To my surprise, Tasha leaned towards me, and took another sip of her drink. Why she thought I cared, I don't know, but she was definitely doing it to get under my skin, which is why I didn't give her a reaction. I just looked at her like the fool, she was acting like. There was no way, I was wasting my precious energy, on a stupid argument. Especially, since I didn't even know what she was upset about.

"You know what your problem is?" She said, with a grin on her face.

"You're desperate. You're simply too damn desperate. You're always looking for someone to love and comfort you. But, you never think about anybody else. I'm tired of being your free sounding board. You need to start paying me to listen to your dumb ass problems.

At this point, I didn't understand why we're friends, if she felt this way. Yeah, she'd been drinking, but she meant what she was saying. The relief she held in her eyes, told me she had been wanting to tell me off, for awhile. So I wasn't going to stop her. I wanted to know what my so called friend really thought about me.

"And another thing. Darius doesn't give a damn about you, or anybody else. You're just too dumb to see you're dancing with the devil. His ass is crazy, and always has been. Why can't you get that through your thick head. You're like an expensive accessory to him." She said laughing.

"You're just another thing he uses to make other guys around him jealous and envious of his position. How else could he keep up with his large and in charge persona, without any real qualifications or pedigree. He'd just be another nigga with a dream. And stop, talking about this picket fence bullshit too. If he wanted to give you a child, you'd have one by now.

Infuriated, I slapped the solo cup out of her

hand. I wasn't about to let her talk about me, and my baby like she lost her damn mind. I didn't have any idea how to fight. But I was going to beat her ass. I stepped into her personal space. And she bucked back. So we were literally tit-tee to tit-tee.

"Oh. So you think you can whop me Saint Mary?" She laughed, standing inches from my face.

"You can get mad all you want. But believe me. I know what I'm talking about. Actually, now that I think about it. You're not dumb. His ass just has you dick-matized. He still don't love you, though. A nigga will stick his dick in just about anything. So, don't get your hopes up. He's just taking advantage, because you're a pretty simpleton, that is easy to keep in line."

SCREECH!

The sound of screeching tires and clashing metal, disturbed us. We both spun around, and ran into the front yard. A blue sedan crashed into a parked car up the street. I quickly did a head count. After remembering kids were playing in the yard while we were busy arguing like idiots. Immediately, I noticed DeMarcus was missing.

"DeMarcus, DeMarcus!" I screamed, frantically. Tasha did too.

Gripping my hair, I turned in every direction, but didn't see him. Nikki and Octavia pointed up the street, saying the car got him. Tasha and I, both ran up the street, and found him laying limp on the ground. She fell to her knees, and cried rocking her baby back and forth. My adrenaline was pumping so fast. I didn't cry or ask what happened. Instead, I took off towards the house. I threw Octavia and Nikki in the front passenger seat, and drove back to scene of the accident. I could hear sirens approaching, but I didn't care about them or the people huddled around us. I told Tasha to get in the back with DeMarcus, and she did, without hesitation.

Just like that, everything changed. I didn't even know why Tasha was so mad at me, or why I sat there listening to her insult me, and everyone I love. But none of that mattered now. The only thing I cared about was taking care of an innocent little boy, who was injured, in my back seat. I had to do everything I could to make sure he was okay. I called the hospital on my way over, as I rushed to the emergency room. Silently I prayed for hundredth time today, that everything would turn out alright.

Chapter Seven

As soon as I pulled into the emergency room driveway, they grabbed DeMarcus, and put him on a gurney that seemed to envelop his tiny body. Two medical transporters rushed him behind the emergency room double doors, and instructed us to wait in the lobby. Tasha filled out the necessary paperwork at the front desk, while I watched Nikki and Octavia. Surprisingly, there wasn't a lot of people waiting along side us. The girls played with toys and books laid out for kids in the middle of the room. They both asked about their little brother, but were oblivious to the severity of the situation. I tried to watch the television hanging in the corner of the room, but the day's events kept preventing me from processing what was on the screen.

I couldn't stop thinking about DeMarcus, and how he wouldn't be in this situation, if I had left Tasha's house when I wanted to the first time. Now that I think about it, Tasha wouldn't be a complete mess right now, and we probably wouldn't have fought, if I had just stayed home.

She finished up at the front desk, then sat down several sits away from me. I wanted to be there for her, because she hadn't stopped crying since they took him back. Our argument shouldn't have been relevant now, but apparently it still was, because neither of us said a word to each other after they whisked him away. I didn't initiate a conversation, because I had no desire to over step my bounds. I figured she purposely created a large space between us because she didn't want to be bothered with me. Still, I wasn't going home until, I knew DeMarcus was okay. Whether she liked it or not. So I bit my nails, and waited nervously for the hospital attendee to invite us back. She was definitely wrong for what she said to me earlier, but I wasn't going to make a big deal out of the situation. Since I couldn't imagine being in her position. If my child got hurt on my watch, I wouldn't be able to forgive myself.

"Tasha Stewart." A burly woman said, entering the waiting room.

Tasha wiped away her tears, and took the girls hands. I was only a step behind them.

"What are you doing?" She said, glaring over her shoulder at me.

"What am I doing? She couldn't be serious. I want to support you, and make sure my nephew is okay."

Tasha let go of the girl's hands, and spun around on her heels. "After all I said today. You still don't get it. Everything isn't about you. Fatima. Nothing happened to you. My son is the one that is hurt. You don't belong here. His not your child, nephew, or anything else. I don't want your help. Just leave.

Your Ms. Do Right attitude is annoying as hell, and not needed."

I looked to my left and right in disbelief. She couldn't be talking to me. When the hell, did I become her enemy. I had no interest in being the center of attention. I dedicated several of my days off to taking care of her kids, especially DeMarcus. Every part of me wanted to act a fool. But how could I? Technically I wasn't family. I loved Tasha and her kids. For years I considered them my family. I bought them things, babysat whenever she needed, and drove her around whenever her car broke down. But apparently, I was just some idiot she was taking advantage of and using.

"Excuse me ma'am. Can I speak with you for a moment?" The attendee asked, interrupting her speech. She pulled her aside to talk. I couldn't make out what she was saying, because she held a clip board in front of her mouth, and spoke softly. However, I could get the gist of the conversation, by piecing together Tasha's responses. Apparently, DeMarcus needed a blood transfusion. From what I could gather. Apparently, Tasha and the girls weren't a match. It sounded like the attendee was suggesting, I stay and get tested. I volunteered myself, just in case my hunch was correct.

"I'll give you whatever you need, if it will help DeMarcus."

"Bitch are you dumb. Get the hell out of here. I got this. Just leave." Tasha grabbed the girls, and pushed passed the attendee.

Defeated, I drug myself to my car in the emergency room parking lot. I was dumbfounded by how she was treating me. My mind was such a convoluted mess, I just stared blankly as people went in and out of the sliding glass doors. I thought about calling Darius, but I didn't want to hear about him and his endless list of problems. So I decided against it. He had been blowing up my phone the entire time, I was at Tasha's. But I kept sending him to voice mail. The last thing I wanted to think about was getting myself into another complicated situation. When I was already in the middle of an argument.

"What the hell is going on?" I said aloud, perplexed.

Quietly, I stepped out of my driver's side door, and slowly closed it behind me. Then, I bent down, and made my way around the car. It had been several hours since we arrived. There were only a few cars in the parking lot, and most were occupied by hospital staff. The parking lot was dimly lit. I squinted, and attempted to look around the line of bushes standing next to my car, but couldn't see very well. I needed to move in closer. I camouflaged myself as best I could, and moved through the lot like a highly skilled ninja. If my eyes weren't playing tricks on me, there was a Darius look-a-like entering the hospital. When I watched him jog through the emergency room entrance, negative thoughts immediately bombarded my mind. But I shook them off. It couldn't have been him. I had to be tripping. What reason would he have to be here?

"What the hell!" I yelled, and shot up from my hidden ninja pose. The bottom of my jeans got soaked by the irrigation system hiding underneath the bushes. Of course it would randomly come on with me standing here. I couldn't help thinking God was being extra funny today. I shook my pants legs, and beat the excess water of my shoes. I needed to get a better look without being seen. I crept to the side of the building, then peered through the slit between the emergency room curtains, just in time to see Tasha running through the back room doors. She really looked awful. Her eyes were swollen and red rimmed. Her usually whipped hair was matted and scattered in the back of her head. Right away I realized, I probably looked no better, after fighting and worrying all day.

Tasha threw her arms around the Darius look-a-like's shoulders, and my breath got caught in my chest. As I watched the two embrace for what felt like forever, beads of sweat began to form around my hairline. I could feel my blood beginning to boil, as I thought about what I could be witnessing.

Could this stranger, holding my so called friend, be my Darius? I tried to push down the emotions rising in my throat, but it felt impossible. Maybe this was the reason, she was being so cruel to me earlier, and didn't want me to stay. After the day I had, I didn't want to rush to conclusions. I needed solid evidence, not a hutch. What could I do to verify it was him? Obviously, I could go in there, but I wasn't about to start up another fight with her. What if I was wrong. Then I'd feel sad, mad, and guilty. I certainly didn't need anymore stress or upset. I got it. I'll search for his car.

My heart quietly begged me to let it go. Darius and Tasha together. It couldn't be possible. I would have known. There was no way, they could have been together without me catching wind of it. Regardless, of my emotional desire to stay in the dark, my mind wouldn't let it go. I was on a mission to catch his ass, if it was him. I was tired of being everybody's fool. As a walked around the lot, I called his phone. It rang a couple of times, then went to voice mail. It's 12 o'clock in the morning. His tail should be home. To my horror, I saw what looked like his 2012 Audi A8. It couldn't be his. I dialed his number again, and slowly stepped towards the side of the black sedan.

"Damn." I wailed to the top of my lungs it was him. I chucked my cell phone through the driver side window, and the alarm began to sound. A tall fat white man yelled in my direction. So, I grabbed my phone and jetted towards my car. How the fuck could he do this to me, after everything I've done for him. How could Tasha, my girl, betray me. I'm such a fool. I hopped in the front seat, revved my engine, and sped out of the parking lot, before the sloppy man could reach me. I was tired of playing the fool. I grabbed my rear view mirror, and saw the pain and misery in my eyes. Silently, I promised myself, never again.

Chapter Eight

I hadn't been home since I found out the news. Instead I paid for a three day room at the The Renaissance. Plus, I turned off my phone. Quit my job. And popped a few pills since finding out my so called life was an incestuous cluster fuck, I created in my naive mind. Darius my fiance, let alone husband? What a fucking joke. To think I actually wanted to have kids with such a piece of shit was both pathetic and disgustingly hilarious. The lies we tell ourselves.

And that bitch, Tasha, was lucky I didn't drag her ass out of the hospital, and into the street. Hurt child or no. She deserved to get her ass beat. As much as I didn't want to admit it. She was right about Darius. She had his crusty ass pegged. If he wanted to marry me, he would have. If he wanted to make me happy. He would have given me the only thing I ever asked for, a child. I took another swig of my drink, and laughed. I had been doing that so much lately, my sides hurt. It was utterly amazing, how bad things had gotten. He actually chose her over me. The bitch had three kids by three different men, and one of them was mine. I never would have thought. Her pussy literally had no bounds.

Yeah. He claimed me in the street. Bought me things. And on the surface treated me nicely which actually makes it works. Because when I reminisced about the times he said, he wanted to start a family, my fingers start to itch from my bullshit allergy. They itched because every part of me wanted to shot, and stab his ass for every lie he ever told me. To think, he wanted me to help him stay out of jail. The nerve. Meanwhile, he freely Tasha the one thing I wanted the most. There was no way in hell, I was helping his sorry ass. When I thought about bending over backwards to accommodate his needs, and more, I was glad I didn't bring a child into the world. How could I protect a child, if I couldn't even protect myself from these monsters out here today.

I bet his deceitful ass was freaking out, because he couldn't find me. What would he do without his pretty simpleton, as Tasha put it. Now wonder he had no problem asking me to sleep with his brother. He was fucking my soul sister the entire we were together. Why not keep it in the family even more! Them being together explains why she was so happy to hear he flipped out the day Tool called about Eddie threatening to snitch. Her mouth said one thing, but her eyes were jumping with joy when I explained how my nose got busted.

Everything made sense. Tasha knew Darius was a match. Why else would he have been there? They needed his father's blood in order to give him a transfusion, asap. That stupid bitch, knew who his father was all along. Who would concoct a whole story about an imaginary baby daddy who's married with two kids. She was just as sick as his ass.

"Ho? Whatchu doing?" Shana slurred, jarring me out of my thoughts. She stumbled over with Trina and Denise. They all walked across the club to our table. "You came out to party." Shana said, pointing at me. "So come on." She threw her hands up, and started dancing with the others girls.

I didn't want to join. So, I smiled and continued to sip on my drink. I'd been partying with them for the last 24 hours. Every once in awhile we'd chat on Facebook about the wild times we had in college. Shana was the life of the party back in the day. She could get us in the VIP section at any club, and was infamous for streaking down the dorm room halls every time midterms and finals came around. It was like a tradition. Denise on the other hand, was almost the complete opposite. She could be a real drag, but she served a purpose. Some would call her human man repellent. We never had to worry about being swarmed by men. She naturally kept them away. Denise could throw down, and was known for putting bitches to sleep, if things got out of hand. Trina wasn't an old friend. So I couldn't say much about her. All I knew was she gave me Tasha on dubs. As soon as we met, she was telling me about her sex escapades in a climatic fashion, which was enough to turn me off to her. I didn't want another loose trick in my life. One was too many. I hardly said anything to her the entire time we'd been out. I just rolled my eyes, and looked elsewhere, when she started talking.

Out of no where, she yanked me out onto the dance floor. I was too lit to resist. So off I went. She grabbed my waist, and started rubbing her body up against mine. "Get off me." I protested, brushing her off. But she kept popping and dropping various parts of her body. She must have lost her mind. I walked away, but I could fell her on my heels. What the hell did she want?

"Hey, what up." I ignored her, and kept walking. I slid into the booth, and she did too.

"Did I do something wrong?" She asked, wrinkling her forehead.

"I don't know you." I asserted.

"Exactly. Why have you been throwing shade all night, then? You'd think I fucked your man."

"You did." Fell out of my mouth before I could catch the words.

"Is your man Steven?"

"No."

"Q?"

"No."

"Kenny?"

No." I said, throwing my hands up. This girl was already giving me a headache, and this was our first real conversation. At this rate, I better say something, because we'd be here all night, with the amount of men she was naming off.

"How long ago are we talking?"

"You didn't sleep with my man. I don't think you have anyway. You just remind me of someone who did. Recently." I could feel my cheeks heating up on my face. I'm sure she thought I was crazy blaming her for something another female did. If she did think I lost my mind, she didn't show it. But she did start flagging Shana and Denise over. They both staggered over to join us.

"This better be good." Shana said rolling her eyes. She'd been grinding on the same guy all night. It looked like there were heading for the door, as soon as Trina called her over.

"Our friend here has a problem. Trina said, pointing at me.

"Our friend. You'll just met. But what's up." Denise retorted. You could always count on her pointing out the negative, in all situations.

"Yeah. Friend. I said it. Trina raised her brows, waiting for a response, but Denise just sucked her teeth and listened. "She needs our help cashing a whop ass groupon. Her so called girl fucked her man. We should hit her up. Like we used to do tricks back in the day."

All three of them started getting hype. Denise looked especially excited. Any reason to through down was a good reason in her book. I didn't plan on paying Tasha any visits. Doing things like that wasn't part of my style, or personality. But neither was quitting my job, popping pills, clubbing, or half the shit I planned on doing next. Finding out about Darius and Tasha, really fucked me up.

"Who's driving?" Shana said, bouncing her shoulders and throwing her fist.

"I haven't been drinking that much. I'll drive." Trina said, volunteering.

"If we were going anywhere else. I wouldn't have agreed on letting her drive. But oh girl, had a plan to get my self respect back. So how could I deny her. Besides, I had been drinking all night. My car would have been safer in the hands of anyone's, but mine. We were out the club and posted up a few houses down from Tasha house in a hot second. Trina hit the lights, and we quickly began planning.

"I'll throw shit at her car to sound the alarm. Then, one of you grab her ass." Trina suggested.

"That won't work. She doesn't have a car with an alarm. Her old Honda Civic is only for decoration. It hasn't started up since Jesus was walking." I replied.

"Y'all are over thinking this shit." Shana jumped out the car, and the other two girls followed closely behind her. I crept cautiously behind them, questioning my decision to come out here. It was late, and I really wasn't trying to get arrested. Shana knocked on Tasha's door, then took off towards the side of the house. We all followed her lead. The lights in the living room came on. It was game time. As soon as she opened the door, Denise was on her ass. She had her in a head lock, while Shana and Trina got some licks in. My ass was frozen in place. What the hell did I let myself get into.

"Bitch you better throw a blow." Trina said, egging me on. "This is for you. She didn't fuck my man." Tasha was crying and screaming for them to let her go. I can't lie. I loved seeing her in pain. The bitch deserved it after all she put me through. They stopped hitting her, and she fell to the ground. I got in a few kicks, before spitting on her curled up body. She was in the fetal position. The neighbors lights came on, and we all jetted towards my vehicle laughing. Trina hopped in the front seat. I sat in the passengers side, and the other girls climbed into the back. What the hell was wrong with me? I just jumped someone, I considered family. And it felt so good.

Chapter Nine

Before I could turn the key and press against the door, it flung open. Darius swept me into his large arms and spun me around the living room, as soon as I stepped through the threshold. He was squeezing me so tight it felt like my rib cage was going to burst.

"Oh my god, baby. I've been going out of my mind. Where the fuck have you been? I couldn't eat or sleep. Every time I tried, I pictured you hurt or dead behind some dumpster. I'm so happy you're home." He voice was so high pitched and filled with concern. You would have thought he actually cared about me. Good thing I knew better than to take him at his word. He put me down, swept the curls away from my face, and looked deeply into my eyes. He obviously wanted to know where I'd been. But I wasn't going to give him any respect by answering his questions. He didn't deserve it.

"Well, I'm back. So you don't have anything to worry about." I said, throwing my keys and purse onto the couch. He looked ragged and weighed down with worry. Who would have thought the shoe would be on the other foot so soon. I walked passed him, and into my master bathroom. I desperately needed to wash up after partying nonstop for the last few days. Turning the shower head on, I saw him enter the bathroom by way of my peripheral.

"So you're just going to stroll in here after being gone for the last five days like nothing happened?" He was pissed. I could see a thick vein pulsating on the side of his temple. Oh well. Those are breaks, I thought to myself. I wasn't about to tell him shit. After the lies, he'd been throwing at me during our entire relationship, he didn't deserve an explanation. Especially not from me.

"What do you mean, baby? I just needed a break from all the stress. Everything is better now." I lied, while slipping off the thin sleeves of my dress, and allowing it to fall onto the floor. I had a surprise for him. I knew he would like. I wasn't wearing a bra or panties. He clenched his teeth and balled up his fist just as I expected.

"What the hell has gotten into you? You've been walking around with your pussy blowing in the wind. You want these niggas out here to see your tit-tees and shit too." I had to throw my hair over my head to disguise the smug grin sweeping across my face. It took everything I had, not to bust out laughing, partially because I enjoyed his pain, and partially because the cush I smoked with Trina hadn't completely worn off yet. No wonder he'd been pulling my strings all this time. It felt good watching him squirm. I bunned my hair and stepped into the shower. I could see him stewing through the glass.

"Fatima. We're gonna talk. I'm not letting you get away with disappearing on me. So do you want to do it, now or later?" He folded his arms and waited. Ignoring him I continued to wash up. I still didn't have anything to say. If he thought I'd be bending to his will, he had another thing coming. If anyone should be answering questions, it was his ass, not me. While washing my hair, I reached behind me and blindly searched for my shampoo bar. Instead, I found his chest. I could recognize every rip and cut on his body, with or without my vision. I probably knew his body better than my own.

"What are you doing in here?" I asked, slightly annoyed.

I knew, he didn't think he was getting any. Not after what I found out. As much as, I wanted him to leave. I still didn't feel like arguing. So I pretended he wasn't there. Darius wasn't the man I thought he was, but I couldn't help still loving him. When he scooped me into his strong arms earlier, it took everything I had inside of me not to melt. Even though, my dream of being his wife, and mother of his children was permanently put on the back burner. I wasn't ready to let him go. Not yet anyway. I tried to get him out of my system by reliving my college days with Shana and Denise. But it didn't work. I still thought about him the entire time I was gone. None of the men that approached me came closing to getting my attention.

"What? You didn't miss this when you were gone?" He said, stepping close behind me as he slid his dick along my lips below.

Instantly, my mind started thinking nothing and everything at the same time. What was he doing? Wasn't he just in the middle of bitching me out. Now all of sudden he wants to fuck? I wasn't prepared for this. I expected him to cuss me out or want to fight, but not this. What was he thinking?

Darius started teasing me by rocking back and forth without taking the plunge. Then he grabbed more than a handful of my breast and squeezed, before twisting and flicking my nipples which was driving me wild. The warm stream of the shower fell between us, and only heightened my excitement. Every part of my mind, said get out! Run away. Danger. Danger. It's not safe here. But, my legs wouldn't move. I was just a helpless victim to the hold he had over me. It was feeling too damn good stop now.

His wet lips landed on the curve of my neck as he peeked his manhood in and out of my honey pot. She was hot, wet, and ready to play. I couldn't help wrapping my legs around his waist. He grabbed my cheeks and beat it up until, I was screaming his name, not caring who heard the pleasure I was in. Damn. I loved being teased. And he knew it.

Just before I was ready to cum, he pulled out and spun me around. My hands slapped against the marble shower wall, before he entered me from behind.

"Do you like that?" He asked through clenched teeth.

"Yes. Daddy. Give to me. It feels so good." I screamed back at him." Pumping away, he said, "Good. I'm glad I've got your attention." Darius pulled out and slammed his nine inch dick into my ass. The pain was so great, I tried to drop to my knees but he wouldn't let me.

"Don't move." He said, while grabbing my throat and thrusting away.

"You brought this on yourself. All you had to do was listen. But you couldn't do that. Instead you wanted to leave and act like a stupid bitch. So now you have to be punished."

He hammered against my body, not caring that he was tearing me apart. My head felt light and dizzy, while every muscle in my body tingled and ached. I wailed for him to stop, but he just went harder. It was like my pain turned him on. Finally, he grunted in relief, before pulling out and allowing me to collapse onto the concrete floor.

"Don't you ever think about leaving again. If you try, I'll kill you. Now get yourself together. That little stunt you pulled put us behind schedule. You still have to get my money. So be ready to meet my brother tomorrow. I've got everything setup." He turned to leave, but then I saw his feet pivot in my direction.

"And if you think I'm playing, try me. I love you Fatima. I really do. But if you betray me again, I'll make this feel like a dream compared to what I'll do to you next." He stepped out of the shower, and left me to cry on the floor. The taste of salt filled my mouth as I balled up on the floor. I couldn't lift my head, let alone my body. I had no energy left. I watched the blood stained water run down the drain, in disbelief. How could I have been so stupid?

Chapter Ten

I hadn't spoken to anyone since what happened last night. What could I say? And to who? There wasn't anyone who gave a fuck about me to call. I couldn't call Tasha. That relationship was trash, since I found out she had a child with Darius. Actually, it was shit much earlier than that. I was just too stupid to realize it. Besides, our chances of savaging any possible friendship died, when I jumped her with Trina and the girls. And I honestly can't say I regret it. I could never look at her the same.

After Darius was done, he left for a few hours. There was no conversation or exchange between us, which I have to say I appreciated. I couldn't handle looking into the void, he called eyes. I still couldn't. It was too much. I knew, I was partially responsible for what happened. He obviously was concerned about where I had been, and instead of telling him, or responding directly, I played games like a child. I should have simply respected his feelings, and cooperated when he requested to talk. But like an idiot, I didn't. So I paid the consequences.

When he came back to my apartment last night, he pulled me into his arms after coming to bed, and kissed me good night. My heart nearly flipped over and out of my chest, when he touched me. Every part of me wanted to jump out of bed screaming.

But I knew better. It would only make matters worse. I fell into a twilight sleep for a few hours, but still had so many questions running through my mind at the same time. Mainly, how could he do what he did to me? I knew he had issues, of course. But I never thought he could hurt me so badly. I truly believed he loved me. Maybe not in the traditional sense, but in his own way. Now I realize, he couldn't possibly care about me, or anyone else. There is no denying, Darius was a devil in men's clothing. The physical pain he put me through was nothing compared to the emotional rot he left in the center of my chest. He knew what I went through growing up in the system, and promised to never hurt me like that. In fact, he swore I'd never go through anything remotely similar to what I experienced in foster care, as long as I stayed by his side. Only to turn around and do the same thing he swore to protect me against. How could he?

"Fatima. You ready?" He asked breaking my thoughts.

"Yeah." I said, staring out the car window, avoiding his eyes.

Darius sat in the drivers side of my black Toyota Camry. He hadn't said much all morning. However he did, pick out my clothes for the day which was a short sundress, a half jean jacket, and pair of brown wedge heels. I didn't care for the combo, but didn't protest. The funny thing was he also made breakfast, and even ran my bath water, as if it would change what he did to me. The drive over to the hospital was quiet, until now. I was looking forward to getting away from him for a few moments. Even though, the last time I was here, I saw him and Tasha together through the emergency room window.

"I know things have been rough for you lately. But I don't want you to give up on us. Couples go through rough patches. This is just one of them." He couldn't have said what I think he said. Could he? A rough patch. That's what he called raping his own fiance. I turned my hips away from him and clung to the passenger side door. This monster wasn't worth talking too. Especially since, nothing I said or felt mattered to him anyway.

"Fatima. I love you. I just needed to make you understand what you did wasn't okay. You get that now right?" His large hand palmed my knee, while I mentally kicked him off of me.

"I know baby. I love you too," seemed like the only way to respond. He proved to me he was limitless. I saw the real him last night. There was no way, I could ever forget who I was dealing with. I sure wasn't going test my chances. I knew I was treading dangerous waters.

"That's my girl … Now go over the game plan we discussed. We can't mess this up. If were still going to get married and have a little baby running around soon." My stomach twisted at the thought of the idea. A baby with him, was the last thing I wanted. I'd get an abortion first.

"Tasha is going to bring DeMarcus. So I can take him to his checkup with your brother. I'm supposed to tell him, Tasha couldn't get off work to take him to his appointment, which is why I'm doing it for her. Then, you want me to ask him out. So I can get closer to him in order to steal his financial information for you." I watched as a happy couple came out of the hospital with their new bundle of joy. Just a few weeks ago, I thought we'd be them soon. Now, I wished we never met.

"I need you to steal his information. So we can have the life we want. This isn't just for me. It's for us. Remember that. This is a team effort okay? Everyone has to play their part." He said, pulling my chin to face him.

"Okay." I agreed, wanting to be anywhere but with him.

"By the way, I know what you did the other night."

"What do you mean?" I asked, trying to figure what trick he was going to pull out his hat next.

"I went to see Tasha the other day, and she was all lumped up. She said it was you and a few other bitches. At first I thought she had to be confused. It couldn't have been you. Like a fool, I defended you to her. Then I saw how you where behaving when you came home, and realized she was telling me the truth."

I could feel a migraine coming on. That bitch never stopped being a pain in my ass. She knew she deserved that ass whopping. It was the only justice I got out of the whole situation. Still, I didn't want to get on his bad side. There was no telling what he would do to me, if I did. I tried to explain.

"Darius I …" I began to speak, but he cut me off.

"You don't have to explain. I know why you did it. Hell, I'd fuck somebody up if they ever laid a finger on you. Outside of this situation, of course. As sad as the circumstances are right now, I understand you may have to give my brother a little pussy in order to keep my black ass out of jail. Even though I understand where you're coming from, I can't have you hitting the mother of my child again. You're my future wife and everything, but I can't have you two fighting. Y'all are going to have to work together. Because if you think about it, technically, the two of you are like family."

He had every fluid in my body boiling. Like family? Me and that bitch were already like family, before his dick got in the way. I couldn't believe what he was saying. I just wanted to get the hell away from him.

"Do you hear me?" He asked, irritated.

"I hear you. It won't happen again."

Tasha pulled up in her beat up Honda Civic just in time, because I was too through with his conversation. Little DeMarcus was looking good from what I could see, but he did have a sling on his arm. We all stepped out and gathered in the parking lot.

"Aunty Fatty." DeMarcus called, running to me with a huge smile on his face.

"Hi baby." I cooed back, I was just as excited to see him. I swept him up while avoiding his arm. Then waited for Darius' instructions.

"Tasha." he probed.

"Hey Fatima." She said sucking her teeth, and rolling her eyes.

"Hey." I said, smirking at her. We really fucked her up. Her left eye was the exact opposite of her high yellow complexion. It looked like a lumpy plum sitting on top of her face. She had random scratches and bruises everywhere from what I could see. I had to admit, I enjoyed seeing her look how I felt.

"I don't want no funny business going on with

my baby." She put her hand on her hip, and positioned herself in front of me. The bitch was trying to intimidate me. Apparently, she wanted more of the other night.

"Cut that shit out." Darius reprimanded her, before I could respond. She knew better than to think I would hurt a child. Even though, I had been acting out of character lately, that part of me would never change.

"You know Fatima loves those kids. I won't let you keep mine or the other two away from her. Y'all are going to learn to love each other, again. This shit is exactly why, I kept everything sealed up. You two are both too selfish to see the big picture."

I ignored them both and played with baby. This nigga was crazy, and Tasha was a basic bitch. So I didn't have anything to contribute to the conversation.

"We'll be back in about an hour. Text me when you're done." He said, pecking me on the lips., They both took off in separate cars.

It felt like we were in the waiting room forever. DeMarcus had fallen asleep ten minutes ago, and my arm was already completely numb. He was a big boy for four years old.

"DeMarcus Stewart."

"Finally."

I gathered my purse before heading to the back. She took his weight, height, and temperature. Then lead us to the examination room where I started sweating bullets. I hadn't dated or thought about a man in three years. Now Darius expected me to seduce one. That was his brother no less. I didn't even know where to start.

"Good Afternoon. Ms. Stewart. I'm Dr. Du Bois. Nice to meet you." His massive hand swallowed my slim fingers. His presence and frame was larger than life, but he had a gentle aura, I couldn't quite place. He began looking over his chart while I rocked DeMarcus back and forth.

While he was reading I couldn't help noticing, he was even better looking than Darius which was really saying something. His skin was rich and dark like the finest marble money could buy. When he smiled his skin and teeth competed to out shine each other, but neither could win. There was no way to pick between them. They were both so beautiful. I was sitting down when he came into the room. But it appeared he was a good three inches taller than Darius, which was an added bonus for an Amazon like me. I had to admit, he was impressive. A tall, dark, and handsome single black doctor was hard to find. Too bad I met his psychotic brother first.

"Ms. Stewart. Are you alright?" He said, waving his hands in front of my face.

"Uh. Yes. I'm sorry … I'm fine." I stammered. "Just a little tired. I'm Ms. Butler by the way. His mother couldn't take off work. So, I brought him instead."

He must have been trying to talk to me the entire time I was ogling his goodies. My throat dried out from embarrassment. I definitely wasn't getting off on a good foot. Marcus asked standard medical questions about his health, and checked his arm. When he examined DeMarcus he was so sweet and lighthearted. He made jokes and gave him a sucker. DeMarcus was immediately asking when he could come back to the doctor again. If that wasn't a sign he knew how to do his job well, I didn't know what was. Watching him, stirred up feelings of regret. I missed my job as a teacher. Even though, it was summer time. I knew I had no job to return when the school year started again. Thinking over the last few weeks, it hit me how much Eddie threatening to squeal ruined my life. Things weren't ever the same after Darius found out.

"Well. It looks like everything is okay. Stacy will setup your next appointment at the front desk." He smiled and motioned towards the door." Shit. I got lost in him, I totally forgot why the hell I was even here.

"Dr. Du Bois." I rushed behind him, unsure of what to say. " Excuse me. I was wondering. Is there a Mrs. Du Bois?" I asked, nervously.

He flashed that handsome of smile of his, and grabbed his chin. At the very least he was flattered by question. "No. It's just me."

"I hate to take up your time. I know you're a busy man." Before I could finish, he put up his hand to stop me.

"Ms. Butler, you really are a beautiful woman. Any man would be lucky to have you. I'm just not in the market right now. But thanks." He gave me a weak smile, then left. Damn. What was I going to do.

Chapter Eleven

As expected, Darius acted like a caged animal when I told him Marcus turned me down. He flipped practically every surface over in the house during his rage. No matter how many different ways I tried to explain he wasn't interested. He kept giving me the same answer. Figure it out. There was only a week left, before Eddie's arraignment. Which meant time was running out fast. It was obvious he was feeling the fire, and as a result, so was I. There had to be a way for me to get close to Marcus. After spending several hours trying to come up with different ways to bump into him, I finally discovered a practical solution. I would literally have to be a little more reckless in my approach.

I pulled into the parking space across from Marcus's vehicle. Perfect. He hadn't left for work yet. Killing time, I grabbed my rear view mirror and double checked my makeup. My lips could definitely use another coat of my favorite red lipstick, Rubywoo. It was like confidence in a tube. I could never go wrong when swiping it on. It was the perfect compliment to my smooth honey complexion.

As I waited, I thought about our visit the other day. Surprisingly, I hadn't stopped thinking about him since. There was something so sweet and mysterious in his eyes. Even though, he smiled and put on a good face, I could tell there was pain underneath it. When I was around him, I felt like we were kindred spirits. He was so tender and patient with DeMarcus. It was refreshing to see a man be so gentle. Being around him stirred something up in my spirit that I can't quite put my finger on. It never occurred to me there might actually be benefits to meeting him. I had dreaded the this day for so long. Especially since Darius wanted me to con him. At first I rejected the idea because I didn't want to be romantic with another man. Now, I didn't want to because Marcus didn't deserve to be another one of Darius's victims. Of course, I wanted to avoid the wrath of Darius at all cost, but spending time with Marcus was no punishment. I just hated the fact, he was a pawn in a sick game.

From the corner of my eye, I could see Marcus leaving the hospital main entrance. I pushed up my girls, nested in my yellow form fitted dress, and prepared to put on my best performance. Backing up, I slammed into the back of his Nissan Altma. The tail light and fender were hanging off, now.

"Hey! Watch where the hell you're going." He shouted, waving arms above his head.

I jumped out of the car, and mocked innocence. "Oh my god. I'm so sorry. I didn't realize how close you were. Can you forgive me?" I inspected the damage I caused accidentally on purpose, while he stood by steaming.

"How the hell couldn't you have seen my vehicle? There's no traffic. It obviously wasn't going anywhere." He was pissed, and not taking the fender bender as well as I hoped.

"Please forgive me. Wait here. I'll give you my policy information." I ran to my car and grabbed want I needed from out the glove box. I checked my side mirror to see if he was watching and he wasn't. This guy wasn't going to be easy to break.

"Here you go." I said, passing my info over.

"Thanks." Marcus headed to his car to leave.

"Wait up." I ran to his side, before he could sit down in the drivers seat. "I was hoping, I could take you out to make up, for my little accident." I said, giving him my sweetest smile.

"Is that what this is about." He said, crossing his arms. "I told you the other day, I wasn't interested. Just let up. Okay."

His tone wasn't mean, but it certainly was final. I had to go home, and tell Darius, I failed. There was no telling what he was going to do to me. All of sudden, I saw myself crying on the shower floor as my blood circled down the drain. The memory sent me into a panic, my heart sank to the pit of my stomach, and I began to cry.

"Hey. Don't do that. Okay. I'm sorry." He said, wrapping his arms around me.

I cried into his chest knowing, tonight would be an encore of what happened the other night. There was no way around it. Darius made it clear, he needed the money to stay out of jail, and I owed him for everything he gave me. One way or anther, I was going to have to pay him back. Marcus rubbed my back until I stopped sobbing into his chest. I'm sure he thought I was crazy now. If he didn't before. The front of his white coat was soaked in my tears, and smeared with makeup, but he didn't seem to mind. He wiped the back of his hand across my cheeks, and gave me a weak smile. I couldn't understand why this man, I was trying to con was being so sweet to me after I intentionally wrecked his car. Deep inside, I knew I didn't deserve his kindness or concern. But it still felt good nonetheless.

"Thank you. I'm such a mess." I said, feeling a mixture of guilt and shame.

"Don't worry about. Are you okay?" His eyes were filled with genuine concerned, which only made me feel worse. I didn't want to do anything to cause this man anymore trouble. I surely didn't want to help Darius. He was a monster, but I knew not doing what he said, only meant more pain and misery for me.

"Yeah. I really am sorry about your car. I'd really like to make it up to you by taking you out to eat." I'm sure I looked as pathetic as I felt. But I had to give it one last shot, before going home.

At first Marcus didn't respond. He just gave me a sympathetic smile. I'm sure the poor guy didn't know what the hell to say. I started to turn towards my vehicle, but he stopped me.

"Saying no to a beautiful woman is hard. But saying no to a beautiful woman in tears is impossible. I'll go, but I can't let you pay. I'll pick you up tomorrow night. Just text me your contact information." He said handing me a card.

I couldn't believe it. He actually agreed, after seeing me wail like an unstable idiot. I wanted to faint, skip, and cry all at the same time. Thank god he agreed to meet me.

*****

We'd been sitting across from each other for at least thirty minutes, but not much was said. My fear was becoming a reality. Marcus agreed to come out with me, but it was clear he wasn't ecstatic. For what reason, I didn't know. I never had a problem attracting men before, but he seemed really uninterested.

"So what made you decide to become a doctor?" I asked trying to stir up conversation.

"Do you want to know the truth, because it's pretty depressing."

I couldn't possibly imagine anything more depressing than sitting here another minute with him in silence. So his question was pretty easy to answer.

"Of course I want to know the truth. It can't be much worse than some of the things I've been through."

"Well. When I was growing up. I had a little brother, Eric. He was a tough little guy. And pain in my ass. But I loved him." Marcus shook his head and stared at his plate. It was obvious he was strolling down memory lane.

"Anyway. He got mangled up pretty bad by a train. I really don't care to get into the details, but I knew I wanted to help kids feel better, after what happened to him."

Looking across the table, I could see sincere pain in his eyes. I hated bringing up unwanted memories. Especially, since Darius already told me about their brother. There was no point, in making him recall such a miserable childhood event. The night was definitely going down hill fast, I had never been on such an awkward date in my life. I desperately needed a drink.

"I don't get out very often. I take it you don't either?" I said trying to lighten the mood.

"Oh can you tell." he said, laughing.

"The last time I went on a date was before my wife died."

He didn't again. The heavy blows just kept on coming. I knew something good must have happened in his life.

"I'm sorry to hear that. What happened?" I really didn't want to hear anything negative, but I'd choose bad conversation over no conversation any day.

"She had just left the school with our daughter, and some careless asshole decided to get on the road drunk. Man. I can't believe that was over three years ago." He shook his head and wore the same expression he did when talking about his brother, before waving down the waitress.

"Can I get a shot of tequila? And whatever the lady wants." He ordered.

"I'll take the same." I was happy to see we were finally on the same page. The waitress brought us our drinks, and we started knocking shots back, one after another, until we were lose enough to speak freely.

"So Marcus?" I said, leaning on the table with my arms pressed against my breasts. "Am I your type?" I genuinely wanted to know, because even though conversation had picked up. He still hadn't made any plays.

He laughed and took another shot. "I don't have a type."

"Bullshit. Everyone has a type. What did your wife look like?"

The smile was wiped clean off his face. It was obvious I caught him off guard.

"You don't have to answer that, if you don't want." I said, trying to clean up the mess I made.

"No. You didn't say anything wrong. She was petite, and blonde."

"Oh." I said, laughing. "That explains a lot."

"What does that mean?"

"It means. You were never interested me, because I'm a black girl. Light, but still black. Not to mention the fact, that I'm tall." Marcus licked his lips and eyed me from head to toe from across the table.

"There's absolutely nothing, I don't find attractive about you. Like I said. I don't have a type. I'm into the whole woman. Not just spare parts."

"Is that right." He certainly piqued my interest. I

wanted to know everything about this mysterious man who healed sick children, survived losing his family, and still managed to be decent.

"Would either of you like another drink?" The waitress asked. Marcus shook his head no. I on the other hand, asked for two additional shots. I was going to have to be loaded in order to screw him over, literally and figuratively.

"Maybe, you should take it easy."

Marcus reached across the table and squeezed my hand. It was clearly his attempt to enhance his words. But what he said didn't matter, because I had already decided to get annihilated before leaving the house. How was I going to steal from this kindhearted person? I already felt bad about what Darius asked me to do, before finding out his wife and child died. He already had so much tragedy in his life. I didn't want to be the reason for anymore.

"When was the last time you made love to a woman, Marcus?" I asked in a sultry voice. I knew, asking him about sex would change the subject. No man could resist listening to his little head. Not even the good doctor.

Marcus cleared his throat, pulled at his collar, and began to sweat. Apparently, it had been quite sometime. "You get right down to business, don't you?" He said, looking around nervously.

I wanted him to take me home. As sad as the situation was I really liked being with him. Maybe it was naive or reckless for me to think we could be together, but I really wanted to see where things could go. Darius had no plans on setting me free. I knew if I helped him stay out of jail, I'd be imprisoning myself. Attaching myself to Marcus was my best bet. If anyone could protect me against Darius, it would be Marcus. He had to know him better than anyone else, which is why I decided to get as drunk as humanly possible. He'd have to take me home then. It was the easiest way to avoid going home to Darius.

Chapter Twelve

After our schizophrenic date, Marcus carried me up the stairs and into his cottage style bedroom. He was the perfect gentleman. When I woke up, I saw him reading in a lazy boy recliner across the room. I looked down and realized I had the same clothes on from the night before. My purse and shoes were stacked neatly on top of the wooden chest in front of his bed. To my surprise, he didn't try to undress or make a pass at me. It was strange and unusual to feel so safe with someone I just met. He smiled and continued reading when he saw I was awake. When I thought about how drunk I got, I started to feel self conscious and insecure. Maybe he took pity on me, and that's why he let me stay. If he felt that way, he didn't show it. In fact, Marcus treated me like a welcomed quest. The entire time we spent together, I found no judgment in his eyes or voice. There was no way he could have been more chill about the situation.

At first, the vibe in his home threw me off. There was no traffic or loud voices outside the walls. Instead, I heard birds, insects, and wild life from his bedroom window. It was strange and amazing. I didn't know where I was, and honestly didn't care. I was just happy to be far from home. He lived miles away from the city, which allowed me to imagine I was a different person living under new circumstances. All Fourth of July weekend – we ate, read, and made love like we knew each other for years. He was so relaxed and out of practice, he allowed me to take control of the wheel, which I desperately needed after my horrible experience with Darius. I have to admit the last couple of days with him read like a passage straight out of a romance novel. If I didn't have a small bomb ticking in the back of my head. I would have thought I died, and woke up in heaven.

I rolled over and smiled at Marcus sleeping beside me. He single-handedly restored my faith in love and life in a matter of days. Who knew, we'd fall for each other so hard. Especially since, I had to beg before he would come out with me. As I watched him sleep a tinge of guilt overwhelmed me. This wonderful man revealed everything to me. Meanwhile I was keeping secrets that could hurt us both.

"Good morning, beautiful." He said, propping up on his elbow while giving me a crooked smile. "How'd you sleep?"

"Better than ever." I replied, placing a soft kiss on his lips. As cheesy as it may sound, I was telling the truth. I've never slept so well in my life. Out here in the boonies life was simple. We were able to spend the entire three day weekend enjoying each other. Since his practice was closed due to the holiday.

"You know today's the Fourth, right? What do you want to do?" I asked, knowing tomorrow was Eddie's arraignment. I had no desire to go anywhere. Because I didn't want to risk bumping into Darius.

"I'm good with staying home. I really don't like the city life. I'd rather spend more time at home with you."

Buzz Buzz Buzz

My cell phone started vibrating on the bed. How the hell did I forget to put it back in my purse? I must have gotten lost in the moment last night. Marcus reached for my phone, before I could. Panicking, I snatched it out of his hand.

"Jesus." He yelled, yanking his hand away from me.

"I'm sorry baby. Let me see." Dammit. I didn't mean to hurt him. Darius had been blowing my phone up since our date the other night. He kept sending me messages every few minutes. I read none of them, because I wasn't going home no matter what they said. Marcus was being so good to me. I hated not being able to tell him the truth. But I didn't know how to explain the situation yet. I needed a little more time. So I avoided the subject all together.

I ran to the bathroom, and got a wash cloth to cover his cut. Unfortunately, I got him pretty good. I dabbed at the broken skin on his hand, even though it wasn't bleeding.

"Fatima. I'm fine. It's nothing. Trust me. I'm a doctor remember."

"I know. I'm just sorry I hurt you, babe." I said pouting.

Sitting on the bed across from each other, I could tell there was something he wanted to say by the way he was studying me. If I wasn't so afraid a bone would fall out of my mouth, I would have asked what was wrong.

"Is there something you want to tell me?"

"No. I don't think so. Should there be?" I feigned innocence and hoped for the best.

"I admit. I've been out of the game along time, but I'm not an idiot."

Dammit. He wasn't going to let up.

"Who was calling your phone? Your husband, boyfriend, friend with benefits? Who?" He looked concerned and a little hurt. I didn't know what to say to relieve his stress. Telling him the truth wasn't going to do it. It would only stress us both out more.

"No. I'm not with anyone but you. Some idiot

keeps calling to speak to Angie. I've told him hundred times, this is not Angie's phone. But he keeps calling."

It was obvious he didn't believe me, but thankfully he let the conversation go. I was off the hook. At least for the moment.

*****

Marcus was in the kitchen cooking up some catfish he caught earlier today. While I went to check the weather on the nightly news in the living room. We had old school rhythm and blues playing in the background, and the entire front room lit up with vanilla scented candles. Sitting in front of the television with a flute of red wine in hand, I could tell tonight was going to be good.

The usual boring stories about politics, sports, and new developments came on before they got to weather. "It looks like tomorrow is going to be a good day for fishing. It's supposed to rain." I yelled back towards the kitchen.

"Thanks babe."

I got up to join Marcus in the kitchen, but the next report got my attention.

"There was a fire located at 555 Parkway

Avenue in the Greenwood Park Addition. Authorities can't say for certain who was caught in the fire. But they suspect the only tenant living there by the name of Darius Du Bois was the unidentified body found badly burned …" The reported continued, but I couldn't hear a word she said. That monster found away to escape the system.

"What's wrong? Is everything okay?" Marcus was cleaning up the broken wine glass, I apparently dropped on his maple hardwood floor. I didn't even realize it fell. While he was knelt down in front of the television, I could see he began to listen to the report.

"Hell yeah." He cheered. Karma finally got that bastard. How about another drink? My night just got a whole lot better?" He asked before jogging to the kitchen to get two wine glasses.

Was he actually happy his brother was dead? I felt like I had deja vu. Darius responded the same way after finding out his father was died.

"Here," he said, thrusting a glass of wine in my hand. "Oh, don't look at me like that. That monster was related to me by chromosomes only. You'd understand if you knew what he was capable of." Marcus clinked his glass against mine and took a big swallow. "Thank you Jesus." He said, before running to check on our dinner.

Of course, I knew exactly what Darius was capable of. Or at least I thought I did. What possibly could have happened to make them hate each other so much. According to Darius, he ran away from home after Eric's death, and never saw Marcus again. I had to find out what was going on.

"Bottoms up." I said, joining him in the kitchen. I drank the rest of my wine, and hopped on the counter. "Do you want to share why we're celebrating your brother's death? It's kind of creepy. Don't you agree?"

Marcus rubbed his hands together, then gripped my knee caps. He was clearly excited to share the good news.

"I refuse to admit any relation to it. I can't even standing talking about it. You remember the reason I became a doctor, right?"

"Of course. Your little brother, Eric got hit by a train. So you decided to become a pediatrician."

"That's only part of the story. My brother didn't just get hit by a train. It took him out in the middle of the night, and tied him to the railings. By the time, neighborhood kids found his body it was nothing but cracked bones, torn tendons, and rotten flesh. The bastard came home and slept like a baby. Knowing exactly what he did to my brother. My family never recovered. Both my parents became alcoholics. They stayed together until my dad died.

But they were both like the walking dead after it happened. Things were never the same. The only reason we discovered what it did was because the rope wrapped around Eric's rib cage was still there. That's why I'm glad the motherfucker burned to death."

Marcus looked overjoyed. He wasn't hiding enthusiasm over Darius's mock death. How could I tell him, there wasn't anything to celebrate because the monster was still alive. Feeling sick I excused myself to the bathroom. I had to figure out a way to tell him the truth. Now that Darius was practically the invisible man. There was no doubt in my mind, he'd come after us.

All of a sudden the lights went out in the bathroom. I flipped the switch up and down, but they wouldn't come back on. Out of now where, there was a loud thud and crashing sound from downstairs. I tripped over my feet scrambling to place my ear against the door. Silence. Should I peak my head into the hallway to see what was going on? Maybe he fell or knocked over the television, because he wasn't paying attention. No. He would at least yell, he was okay, right? Suddenly, my phone began to ring. A familiar sinking feeling enveloped my body. Please don't let it be him. This time I checked my phone to see who was calling, 156 unread text messages, flashed across the screen. I opened the newest one and saw it was Darius. See you soon was all it read.

Chapter Thirteen

I traveled further down the blacked out hallway upstairs with my back firmly pressed against the wall. I thought about all possible options, and scenarios. It was possible the power went out naturally for some unforeseen reason. Darius could have nothing to do with it, the loud crash coming from downstairs, or my phone suddenly being out of service. But the chances were slim. Hell. Who was I kidding? The chances weren't slim. The small bumps running over my entire body confirmed what I already knew. He found me.

The floor creaked as I slowly placed my feet against the hardwood floor. Turning the corner, I saw Marcus's bedroom door was open. I'd have to take my chances scaling down the old wood framed window. Reaching the doorway, I saw no one was there. I hurried inside, unlatched the window, and threw my legs over the edge. Looking down, I could see a line of small scrubs beneath my dangling feet. Maybe they'd soften the fall. It was a risk because Marcus parked his car close to the bushes. So things could go bad, or really really bad. I let out a heavy sigh, closed my eyes, and jumped.

AAH!

By the time I realized he was there, my head

snapped back, my body followed, and he was dragging back inside. How the hell did he know I was here? He must have been watching me the entire time. I screamed for help, but the dirt country road stayed quiet and empty. No one turned on a light or pulled back their curtains. It was just the two of us, fighting alone in the darkness. Where was Marcus? Did he kill him? I thrashed at his hands, and bucked like a thoroughbred. There was no doubt, I was fighting for my life. Still, he wouldn't let go.

A raised nail ripped through my calf as he yanked me through the rustic bedroom window. Blood soaked the bottom of my pants as I twisted and bucked, trying to break free. But he was a powerhouse with shoulders as wide as a refrigerator. His towering build was as strong, and stout as any linebacker. Unfortunately, he was aimed at me. I was no match for him. Still, I gave it my all, but it was no use … he had me.

On the way in, the sound of spilled furniture filled the room. Disheveled, I searched for my phone, unable to see anything. I completely forgot it was out of service. My head was so dizzy, and spun out of control, I didn't even realize my mistake. The back of my neck ached, and my scalp felt like it was on fire. I stammered to my feet trying to get his massive hands unlocked from my hair.

"Get the fuck off of me," I roared. I wasn't going to make it easy for him to take me out. This was a kill he'd have to earn. I wasn't some naive and defenseless little boy like his brother..

Darius laughed as he drug me around the dark room. "Look at you," he jived. "I told you, I'd find you. You'll never be free, unless I say so." He kneed me in the back and let go of my hair.

Palming the old wood floor, I saved my face from smacking against it. Propping up on my hands and knees, I crawled around the room searching for the door. The sound of my breathe and thudding heart was so loud, it was difficult to hear, where he was in the room. But the raised hairs on the back of my neck told me he wasn't far away.

You thought you could out smart me?" he growled from across the room. "They can't catch me. I'm the living dead." He cackled. "It's just you and me baby, like the good old days."

His feet raced across the room, just as soon as I found the door. Eagerly I turned the nob and pushed. It was just short of completely opening, but then it slammed back close. "What the fuck?" I screamed. I stood on my knees and reached above my head. Dammit. The chain was latched.

Darius grabbed me by my waist and threw me across the room. My back arched in pain. How could he see me? There wasn't a hint of light anywhere. "You remember my promise don't you?" His stride sent vibrations through the floor board which gave me a general idea of his direction. Using the back of my elbows, I quietly squirmed away from him. If memory served me right, I was only a few feet from the window directly beside the bed. Jumping out of it, was my only viable option.

"Where you going, huh?" He said, pulling me up by the neck of my shirt. "I thought I told you Fatty, it's me and you till the end." Darius threw me on the bed, grabbed my throat, and pulled down my pants. He was going to rape. I swung at his face and neck, but it didn't deter him. My hands were met with something solid and hard, that wasn't his face. Heavy droplets fell onto my forehead. I thought it was his sweat, but soon realized it was my own blood falling from my knuckles.

"Yeah. That's my girl." He said, moaning in pleasure. Despite my best efforts I lost. He was already deep inside me. I wailed for him to stop, but he just kept going. Exhausted and weak, I quit fighting. I couldn't say how long it lasted. My mind took me to another place. I just starred into the darkness around me and left.

RAH AAH!

The sound of man howling, jarred me out of my trance. Suddenly, I realized he wasn't on top of me anymore, and I sat up. It was daybreak. The weak

light of the early morning sun crept into the room,
just in time for me to see Marcus charging towards
him. Darius was standing next to the bed dressed
like a special ops solider. I looked down at my
broken knuckles covered in blood, and quickly
realized I was hammering my fists against the night
vision mask he had covering his face. Caught off
guard, Marcus sent him careening out the bedroom
window. I jumped out of bed, and ran towards
Marcus. I wanted to make sure he was okay. There
was a tourniquet wrapped tightly around his neck,
and both of his eyes were swelled shut. There was
no question, he gave Darius a good fight. He
knuckles were swollen and busted like he'd been
beating a brick wall. We both limped to the window
and looked outside, but Darius was no where in
sight. Marcus immediately bolted downstairs hot on
his trail. In horror, I dropped to my knees, and
wailed in disbelief. I couldn't believe he got away.

www.ingramcontent.com/pod-product-compliance
Lightning Source LLC
Chambersburg PA
CBHW070631130626
46555CB00006B/2524